A
Harlequin
Romance

THE BENEVOLENT DESPOT

by

ELIZABETH ASHTON

HARLEQUIN BOOKS

Winnipeg • Canada   New York • New York

THE BENEVOLENT DESPOT

First published in 1970 by Mills & Boon Limited,
17 - 19 Foley Street, London, England.

Harlequin Canadian edition published December, 1970
Harlequin U.S. edition published March, 1971

Standard Book Number: 373-51453-0.

Printed in Canada

CHAPTER I

The last of the summer twilight was deepening to dusk as Pauline Herald led her truant horse down the lane between a low bank on the one hand, and a hedge on the other, over which the scent of honeysuckle lingered. In the dim light only the girl's light blouse and pale face showed, the horse was a dark shadow moving beside her. Pegasus had broken out of his paddock, and she was thankful to have retrieved him before he had been able to damage either himself or someone's property. But she had little else for which to be thankful, and as her thoughts reverted to her problems, the ready tears rose to her eyes. This hour between day and night always seemed to her to be full of melancholy and the metaphorical night into which she would soon be plunged, when the creature she was leading and which she dearly loved would be torn from her, was looming painfully near.

It was not often that she could give rein to her grief; surrounded by her family, she had to assume some sort of cheerfulness, since she was the eldest and her young brother and sister looked to her for comfort and support. The burden was a heavy one for a girl who had only just attained her majority and had hitherto led a sheltered and uncomplicated life, which had come to such an abrupt and catastrophic end with her father's death in a car accident.

None of them, not even Aunt Marion, who had looked after them since their mother died soon after Lynette's—the youngest—birth, had had any idea that for years they had been living on the brink of bankruptcy, which John Herald had only managed to stave off by mortgages on his property and borrowing heavily from the Bank, and that the riding school which he had started some years back was not a paying proposition. The optimistic schemes he had dreamed up for its development had never reached reality, the covered yard for indoor training was never built, the pupil teachers they were to engage at high premiums materialized into one young woman, who, on her second day, let a horse down, and after the ensuing row, when she met the full blast of John Herald's temper, she had packed her bags forthwith and demanded her money back. Pegasus was to be trained to be a show jumper, but that too had proved a pipe dream, since he too would have to go with everything else to pay her father's debts; even their furniture would have to be sold.

She ran her hand caressingly over the warm neck of the horse—Pegasus, whom she had known throughout his tempestuous career since the day he had been foaled. He was amenable only to herself and her brother Michael. What would become of him ? Into what brutal hands might he not fall, which would seek to break his proud spirit by force, when he could only be tamed by love ? Her tears spilled down her cheeks, and she made no effort to check them. It did not mater, there was no one about to witness her distress.

They had reached a bend in the road, not far from their own gate, when a wide arc of light swathed the dusk, resolving itself into the headlights of a car, which had turned off the maid road into the lane, and was coming towards them. As they rounded the bend, they became illuminated like figures on a darkened stage picked out by a spotlight. Pegasus planted his feet firmly in the middle of the lane and threw up a startled head. She had much ado to keep hold of his headstall, while there was a screech of brakes being hastily applied, and a big black car with a silver mascot on its bonnet slid to a halt a bare six yards ahead of them. Its driver opened the door and jumped out uttering a string of highly coloured expletives. He slammed the door behind him and stood staring at them, a tall menacing figure in the gloom.

'You fool of a boy! I might have killed you.'

'I . . . I'm sorry,' she stammered, 'I wasn't expecting anything to come along here so late. Come on, boy,' she backed Pegasus into the hedge. 'I think there's just room for you to pass if you go very slowly, and please dim your lights.'

The stranger said in a changed voice, 'I beg your pardon, I didn't realize I was speaking to a girl, but you startled me. What on earth are you doing wandering about with that great brute without showing a warning light?'

'He'd got loose, and as I said I didn't expect to meet anything along here at this hour, and yours is rather an outsize in cars.'

The stranger looked apprehensively at Pegasus, who was showing the whites of his eyes. He turned back to his car and switched off his headlights, but not before he had seen Pauline's tear-streaked face.

'I think you'd better try to pass me,' he said, 'if that creature won't kick my paint to bits, but first tell me if I'm on the right road. I'm looking for Barton's Garage in the village of Mullings. Is this Mullings?'

'It is, but you should have kept straight on, not turned up here. It's at the top of the hill, past the Inn.'

'I was told to turn left.'

'Yes, it is on the left, but a little further on.'

He had his back to the lights, so she had not seen his face, but his voice was attractive, low and pleasant and beautifully modulated.

'Is there anywhere further on where I can turn?'

She looked dubiously at the long length of the car. 'Not for some way, but if you reverse you'll come to a gateway, you can turn there. If you do that, we shan't have to pass you.'

He again glanced at Pegasus. 'I think that's an excellent idea.' But he did not move.

'Well then?'

'Forgive me,' he said gently, 'but I don't like leaving you like this. You seem in some sort of trouble.'

So he had seen her tears. She said sharply:

'It's not your business, but anyone in the village will tell you before you've been here five minutes that I've lost my father and my home, and all I possess, including this—' she laid her hand on Pegasus's neck and her voice quivered, 'is going to be sold by auction in a couple of weeks. You'll see the sale notices everywhere—there's one on Barton's Garage.'

'I say, that's tough luck,' he sounded genuinely concerned.

'It's not your tragedy,' she said bitterly. 'And now, having satisfied your curiosity, perhaps you'll be good enough to back your car so we can get home.' Again her voice quivered on the last word as she remembered it would not be home for either of them much longer. Still the stranger did not move.

'I'd like to hear more about this sale,' he began.

'You can get all the particulars from the agent,' she told him.

'Why, so I can,' he said. Actually he already

8

had them. In the silence that followed he seemed to be thinking, while Pauline waited patiently, aware of a curious expectancy. A white mist was rising from the meadows on her left sloping away to the stream below them, the night was full of summer scents, roses, honeysuckle and gorse, and very still, even on the main road, traffic had ceased, above them the stars were beginning to shine, and low down in the west a faint amber glow marked the place where the sun had set; only the side lights on the car struck an alien note. Then from the trees above the hedge, an owl hooted. Pegasus took this for a signal to make his protest; he wanted his stable and his supper. He pulled at his headstall and began to dance; the stranger retreated hastily.

'Right, I'll get moving,' he said, and re-entered his car.

Pauline was vaguely disappointed. What she had expected she did not know; her troubles, as she had said herself, meant nothing to this stranger, but she was still young enough to believe that some miracle might happen to prevent the catastrophe. The return of a wealthy and forgotten relative from America, all the possibilities popular fiction suggested, had occurred to her, and this meeting was linked with her hopes, but it seemed it was only a chance encounter after all. The car backed slowly down the lane until it reached the gateway, which was in fact the side entrance into the yard at Three Chimneys, whither the girl and horse were bound. Even there it was a difficult manœuvre to turn the car about. When at length it was accomplished, he cut his engine as she came alongside.

'You can pass now.'

'Thanks, I don't need to, this is my way.'

9

Pegasus, seeing his hopes realized, quickened his steps and Pauline had difficulty in restraining him while she opened the gate.

'Goodnight!' she called, as she shut it behind her.

Three Chimneys was a long, low house built of brick, mellowed by age. It faced south and along its frontage there ran a glass-covered verandah which housed a vine; all of the three front rooms had access to it by French windows. The drive up to the house curved like a horseshoe with a gate at either end leading into the main road. Within its circle was a lawn with a weeping willow in its centre. To the right of the house was a walled garden, to the left a paved way led to the stabling; behind the house the grounds sloped upwards and were terraced to form, first, a rose garden and then a tennis court, terminating in a paddock. A stretch of orchard reached from behind the stables alongside the garden up to the paddock. There was still a profusion of fruit and flowers, but everything was neglected and overgrown, for during his last years John Herald could not afford a gardener, and neither he nor his children had time or inclination for gardening.

Having with her brother's help finished her evening chores, Pauline washed her face and went to join the family in the living room; this in modern parlance was the lounge, the middle room of the three; besides the French window on to the verandah, an archway on the left gave access to the front door and the stairs, and the smaller room they used as an office. On the right another door led into the big room that Aunt Marion still referred to as the drawing room, at the back, a sliding door connected it with the kitchen quarters. The room was square and low-ceilinged and though the furniture was shabby it had once been good. A vase of late roses filled the hearth, and another was on the centre table, placed there by Lynette, the youngest Herald, who loved flowers, and their fragrance filled the room.

Pauline sat down on the oak settle which stood against the back wall, she was still wearing her jodhpurs and blouse, in which she looked more like a boy than a girl; her short curly hair, of a colour between brown and copper, looked burnished where it caught the light, she had wide grey eyes under dark brows, small features and a well cut but obstinate mouth.

At the table, Aunt Marion—she was really their great-aunt—was sorting through a pile of mending, clucking distressfully over the numerous rents and holes in shirts and socks. Marion Thorne had kept house for John Herald for most of the children's lifetime. Although she was a good deal younger than her sister, their grandmother, and was still vigorous, she was beginning to feel the weight of her sixty-odd years, and would not be altogether sorry to relinquish her arduous duties at Three Chimneys. Opposite to her Lynette was darning socks. She was sixteen years old, and had a sweet pensive face, and the same colouring as her sister. Polio in early youth had left its mark upon her, she was still slightly lame and her delicacy had excluded her from attending the various boarding schools which Pauline and Michael had from time to time graced—or disgraced. Shy and retiring, she lived in a world of her own fantasies, coloured by her favourite romances. The only remaining male of the Herald family lounged against the mantelpiece, hands in his breeches pockets, discontent marring his handsome face. Michael Herald was nineteen years old, and thought the world owed him a living until he had been painfully undeceived. At his feet a large golden retriever lay, watching them all with sad brown eyes.

Marion said in her precise well-bred voice, ' I've heard from my friend Agnes by the afternoon post, and she will be only too pleased to have Lynette and me to live with her. She will be retiring soon and with our joint pensions we can manage comfortably, giving occasional lessons for pocket money—' Marion had been a teacher in her youth at the same school as her colleague Agnes Moore—' she says she can take Duchess too—' the dog looked up and wagged a plumed tail, hearing her name, ' but she only has a small flat, and I'm afraid she can't accommodate anyone else.'

' So Lina and I are to be thrown out into the cold, cold world, to sink or swim,' Michael said sullenly.

' Don't put it like that,' his aunt besought him. ' I'll do all I can to help, but you know my resources are small, and after all, you're both young and strong.'

' Of course we are ! ' Pauline threw a reproachful look at her brother. ' You've done more than enough for us, Auntie, we can fend for ourselves.' She wondered vaguely why she was not more fond of her aunt, but Marion had always been aloof, and though now mellowed by age, she had the teacher's bossy manner which had often infuriated her nephew-in-law during his lifetime, but she had given them all patient and faithful service, and John had known very well that it would have been difficult to find anyone else who would put up with the Herald temperament.

' Mike and I will have to get jobs,' Pauline said

firmly.

'What as? We aren't trained for anything.' Michael pointed out.

She hesitated. 'Grooms?' she suggested.

Michael laughed scornfully. 'There isn't a great demand for grooms, most riding schools prefer apprentices, they're more profitable. Besides, I want to do something with cars.' He looked at Pauline pointedly. 'If only you could manage to make up your mind to marry George Barton, he'd give me a job and both our futures would be assured.'

'Won't he give you one without involving me?' she asked.

'No, he knows me too well, but he'd feel bound to help a brother-in-law. You're the sugar that coats the pill.'

'Oh really, Mike! Anyway, what makes you think George wants to marry me?' Uneasily she feared confirmation of her own suspicions. George, the owner of the garage on the hill, was running a prosperous business, they had known him all their lives and she was aware that he cherished tender sentiments towards her.

'It sticks out a mile,' Michael retorted, 'only you always snub the poor brute.'

Lynette said, 'I don't know why you want to have anything to do with cars, after . . . after . . .' her voice trailed away and her eyes filled with tears.

'You mean because Dad smashed himself up in the Mini?' Michael's voice was hard. 'Best thing he could have done. He must have known the crash was coming and he got himself out of the mess.'

'Michael, don't talk like that!' his aunt said sharply, while in her turn, tears rose to Pauline's eyes, the ready tears that always seemed ready to fall since her father's death. She had adored him, he had always spoiled her, though he had never put himself out in any way for his children. He had been a dashing and romantic figure in his youth, whose exploits in the hunting field had won for him the soubriquet of 'Mad John Herald', which title had descended upon his offspring in their turn, the neighbourhood designating them the 'mad Heralds'. It was an irony of fate that John, who during his lifetime had broken practically every bone in his body at some time or other, hunting or breaking horses, had met his death in a car accident.

Aunt Marion looked disapprovingly at Michael; he had always been the most obstreperous of the three, and quite beyond her control.

'You could join one of the Forces,' she suggested. 'A bit of discipline would do you a world of good.'

A look of distaste crossed Michael's face. Discipline was not a popular word with the young Heralds.

'I'd much rather be a mechanic, but George won't play unless Lina bribes him with her lily-white hand, or more correctly her brown paw. He thinks I'm a layabout.'

'Perhaps he isn't far wrong,' Pauline said sharply, while Lynette was shocked. 'Oh, Mike, Lina couldn't marry George if she doesn't love him,' she cried.

'Of course she could, you romantic little nit. Heaps of women marry for a home and security, which is just what Lina needs.'

'I don't,' Pauline declared. 'I'm not decrepit, I'll find something to do, don't you worry.' At twenty-one she did not need to consider security, she thought; life was a challenge and an adventure.

'Anyway, what've you got against George?' Michael persisted.

'Nothing. He's a good sort, and it wouldn't be fair to marry him for what he could give me. He deserves someone who loves him.'

'The slop you women talk!' Michael exclaimed.

'You can't expect Lina to marry George just to give you a job,' Aunt Marion said disapprovingly.

'And anyway he hasn't asked me,' Pauline concluded the discussion, 'and possibly he never will.'

She hoped very much he would not. She liked George Barton as a friend, but as a man he left her cold. To have to refuse him would be a painful experience, which she wished to avoid. She thought that she had made her sentiments sufficiently clear for him not to want to invite a rebuff. She had had enough emotional upsets during the past few weeks without including one with George.

But George's mind was running along the same groove as Michael's. Pauline Herald, happy, playing with her riding school with a secure future ahead of her, was, he had long realized, unobtainable. He was a modest young man and knew that he had little about him to attract a pretty girl. Ruddy-faced, inclining to stoutness which would overtake him in middle life, he had sparse ginger hair, which barely covered his round head, and when shaving, he would ruefully survey his slightly bovine countenance, telling himself it was hopeless to imagine Pauline would ever see him in a romantic light. The small brown eyes under his sandy brows were honest and kindly, but those were not attributes which would stir a young girl's fancy. But Pauline disinherited and homeless was a different proposition, and he knew better than she did how unfitted she was to face an indifferent world on her own.

The son of a prosperous farmer, his inclination, like Mike's, was towards machines, and since his elder brother would have the farm, his father had set him up with his beloved garage, which, since it had a good position on a main road, was fast developing into a flourishing concern. He lived in a bungalow built alongside his sheds and pumps, a modern and comfortable affair which he had begun to hope would one day be Pauline's home.

He saw her passing the morning after he had been the subject of the discussion between Pauline and her brother, she was walking along the highway carrying a basket, intent upon buying eggs and vegetables from a farm a mile along the road. Guessing her errand, he ran out to intercept her.

'If you're going to Crabbe's farm, I'll give you a lift.'

She stopped; she was wearing a faded cotton frock which made her look like a child.

'Thank you, George, but don't bother, the walk'll do me good.'

'It's no bother, and it's quite a step. My car's here.' He indicated a white Anglia, while he whistled to one of the boys he employed to fill a green Austin that had just pulled in.

Pauline wavered. She was tired with the lethargy that had assailed her ever since the shock of her father's death, and the traipse along the road on a warm day was not inviting, besides which, she was pushed for time, and she had work waiting to be done at home.

'It's awfully good of you—unfortunately my bike's punctured.'

'Not at all. Hop in, and I'll do your bike for you when I've a spare minute.'

He opened the passenger door for her, and then

she noticed the big black car parked beyond the Anglia with the silver jaguar on its bonnet.

'Where did that come from?'

'The Jag? Oh, that's Anthony's.'

'Anthony?' her brow crinkled. 'Who's he?'

'An old school friend of mine, he's come down from Town for a few days. He—er—came to look me up.'

Pauline was frowning abstractedly at the car, recalling the meeting with the tall stranger who was looking for Barton's Garage. She had no idea that George had such distinguished acquaintances, though she knew he had been to a good school, and some premonition made her feel oddly disturbed by the discovery.

'He arrived last night, didn't he? He asked me the way.'

'Where the deuce did you meet him?' George was looking dismayed.

'In Tavenham Lane. He'd taken the wrong turning, I was leading Pegasus—in fact he nearly made mincemeat of us.'

George left the subject of Anthony with relief to take up that of Pegasus.

'That darned great brute! You oughtn't to handle him, Lina, he's dangerous.'

'Oh rot, I've handled him ever since he was a foal.' She got into the passenger seat of the Anglia. 'You know, George, you don't know anything about horses although you were raised on a farm, but of course farms are all mechanized nowadays.'

'And a good thing too, saves time and money,' George returned, as he climbed into the driving seat. He glanced round furtively as if to reassure himself that someone he did not want to see was not visible and started his engine.

Her business at the farm concluded and her loaded basket on the back seat of the car, they drove down the loke from the farm, but on reaching the road, he turned left, away from Mullings.

'Where are you going?' Pauline protested. 'I must get home, Aunt Marion wants that cabbage for dinner.'

'I won't keep you long, I want to talk to you.' He drove on, looking for a convenient lay-by and, finding what he sought, pulled up under a tree, which threw a welcome shade. Somewhere amidst its boughs a thrush sang lustily. Pauline was blaming herself for accepting the lift; she suspected what was coming and wished she could avoid hurting her companion. He had taken a large handkerchief from his pocket and was wiping his face and neck; he always perspired when embarrassed.

'Look, Lina love,' he began nervously, 'I'm not much good at putting things into words, but . . . er . . . well, I know you're up against it, been having a tough time and all that. You know how sorry I am about it all.'

'Thank you, George,' she said mechanically.

'Any idea what you're going to do, when . . . er . . . ?'

'After the sale? Oh, get some sort of job. Luckily Aunt Marion can take Lynette, and Mike and I can fend for ourselves.'

She tried to speak brightly and confidently and control her trembling lips.

'Yes, well . . .' he mopped his face again. 'Look, Lina, you needn't do anything drastic. I'm quite ready to give you and Mike a home, and Lynette too, so you needn't be parted, if only you'd marry me.'

18

The last words came out in a rush. So here it was, the proposal Michael had suggested, and the generosity of his offer took her breath away.

'Oh, George, we couldn't all sponge on you.'

'But you wouldn't. Mike could work for me, it's about time someone took him in hand and made him work, and I'd count it a privilege to look after Lynette, poor little soul, she's a sweet kid. I . . . I've always thought the world of you, Lina, and I'm doing very well. The place is a regular gold-mine, you'd lack for nothing,' then as she started to protest, he added with sudden dignity, 'Look, Lina, I know I'm not good enough for you, I'm just an ordinary sort of guy, no looks, no polish like . . .' he checked himself and went on, 'I don't believe you think a lot of me, but don't turn me down right away. Think it over. The world is a cruel hard place when you're on your own and you've always been sheltered. I want to take care of you.'

'Dear George, I do think a lot of you, and you're much too good for me. You're one of my best friends, but marriage is rather more than friendship.'

'Friendship's a good basis to build on,' he suggested.

'Yes, but . . .' She shrank from the prospect of a lifetime with George. Good friend he might be, but he was dull, and he had no physical attraction for her whatever. Yet she felt deep gratitude for his solicitude. He patted her shoulder reassuringly.

'Think about it,' he urged, 'and now I'll take you home.'

He turned the car expertly and they completed the short journey in silence. Pauline was turning over his proposal in her mind. If she accepted him, the future of the three of them was assured. He would, she knew, be good to her, too good, and it was not fair to saddle him with her irresponsible brother and ailing sister. Yet she was tempted; as he had said, the world could be a cruel hard place for a girl alone. Then her spirit rebelled. He was right, of course, but life was a challenge and she meant to do more with hers than to tamely settle down as George's wife. Michael could shift for himself and Aunt Marion had promised to care for Lynette. As the car drew up at the drive gate which was kept shut because of possible straying horses, she said firmly:

'It's no good, George, it isn't fair to give you false hopes. I can't marry you.' She turned away, unwilling to see the disappointment in his honest eyes, to look at her dearly loved home. 'It would hurt too much to live so near Three Chimneys,' she went on, 'seeing strangers in possession. I'd much rather go right away.'

'Meaning that you love this place more than you could ever love me? It's only bricks and mortar, Lina.'

'Perhaps,' she sighed, 'but that's the trouble, George. I don't love you, I wish I did, but I'm afraid I could never love you as a wife should love her husband.'

He said a little bitterly, 'Perhaps you could if I could give you Three Chimneys. I wish with all my heart it were possible, but it isn't.'

She laughed shakily.

'If wishes were horses . . .' but the last word recalled the even greater loss—the horses, which too must go. A sudden thought struck her. 'Couldn't you buy Pegasus?'

'No,' he said firmly, 'that I won't do. Sorry, Lina, but apart from the fact that I've nowhere to

20

put him, I'm quite convinced that some day that animal will kill somebody.'

' Oh, really, George ! ' The softness she had been feeling towards him vanished when he attacked her favourite. She turned in her seat and reached for her basket.

' Leave it,' he said, ' I'll bring it.'

She got out of the car, while he collected her purchases and went to open the gate. Turning back, she saw that he was staring up at the notice board beside it, bearing the inscription: ' The Herald Riding School.'

' Somebody might buy the place as a going concern and keep you and Mike on as instructors,' he suggested hopefully.

' Nobody's going to be such a nitwit,' she told him. ' You know as well as I do that it won't bring in a living. Dad tried . . .' her voice died away.

' He wasn't very businesslike,' George said gently. ' He spent more time hunting than teaching.'

' I know, poor Daddy. He'd no patience with the children, and he spent all the fees on inessentials. If only Mike and I had had the sense to join a good club and pass our tests, we'd have been qualified— as it is we aren't likely to be able to find jobs as instructors. I guess I'll have to take a job as a mother's help, and I pity the poor mother.'

' No, Lina ! ' George was horrified.

' Not to worry,' she said lightly. ' As for that,' she glanced up at the board, ' I'll get Mike to take it down. Don't bother to come in, I'll take my purchases.' She took her basket from his slack hands, noticing that he seemed abstracted. ' Goodbye, and thank you for everything.'

She hurried up the curve of the drive out of his

sight, but George was not watching her; he wanted desperately to help her, but did not know how to do so without offending her pride, since she refused to accept the most obvious way by marrying him. He leaned on the gate, still staring at the notice board. An idea was germinating.

CHAPTER II

The next morning Pauline was carrying a half truss
of hay to the stables from a depleted stack, reflecting
that the store of forage was running low, but might
just last over the date of the sale. She carried
the truss on a pitchfork over her shoulder, and as
she approached the stables she caught sight of
George accompanied by a strange man coming into
the yard. She quickened her steps, hoping to
reach her objective before they had seen her; she
had no wish to stop and chat.

'Lina!' She came to an unwilling halt as
George came hurrying towards her. 'Goodness,
girl, you shouldn't be carrying such a load!'

In his efforts to relieve her of the pitchfork, the
hay slid to the ground between them, and she was
more than a little annoyed.

'Don't be stupid, George,' she told him, 'I can
manage it quite well, and now look what you've
done.'

George prodded the truss inadequately. 'Surely
Mike . . . ?'

'No. I do my share of the feeding. I do wish
you wouldn't treat me as if I were a fine lady.
I'll have to do plenty of this sort of thing if I get
a job as a groom.'

George looked at her with the woeful expression
of a chid spaniel.

'Lina, you can't. You mustn't.'

A low amused laugh reminded them that they
were not alone, and Pauline whipped round to
confront the tall man who had accompanied George.

'Lina, this is my friend whom I told you about,

23

Anthony Marsh. Ant, this is Miss Pauline Herald.'

'How do you do?'

She barely touched the hand he extended, as she recognized the voice of the stranger in the lane. Instinctively her other hand went to her hair, which was ruffled and full of hayseeds, her face was hot with her exertions, and her grey eyes were angry at being caught at such a disadvantage.

'We've met before,' she said shortly.

In the daylight she could see that in addition to being tall, he was very good-looking in a dark, aquiline way. He was also impeccably groomed; although he was casually dressed in a shirt and flannels, cut and style were expensive. He was not a boy, over thirty, she guessed; the faint lines about mouth and eyes suggested maturity and experience.

'Yes, you were the kind lady who put me on the right road.' His face softened to a smile which lit up his rather sombre face, and the dark eyes expressed a sympathy he thought she might resent if put into words. Pauline remembered that he had seen her crying and a rush of colour stained her face. She turned with some asperity to George, who, she thought, should have been more considerate than to produce a visitor at such an early hour.

'Please, my fork,' she demanded curtly.

'Let me carry it for you, Lina.' He drove the fork inexpertly into the hay which slithered away from it.

'Please,' she insisted, 'I can manage it, and that hay won't be fit to eat if you go on messing with it.'

'Guess I'm more use with the innards of a car,' he said ruefully. 'I seem to have lost the knack of handling hay.' He surrendered the pitchfork

24

unwillingly.

Pauline gathered the hay together and drove the fork competently through its centre. Lifting her load, she told them that her aunt and Lynette were in the house and went into the stable. To her annoyance the two men followed her, but ignoring them, she went into Pegasus' box, thrusting her load into his rack. He nickered softly when she approached him, nudging her shoulder with his soft nose, then becoming aware of a stranger, started back, flattening his ears and rolling his eyes.

'All right, boy,' Pauline said soothingly, while Anthony stared at the fierce black head with something like horror.

'Is that the animal I met in the lane?'

'It is.' She laid a soothing hand on Pegasus' neck, but he moved away from her, backing up against the wall and snorting.

'For heaven's sake come out of there,' George said anxiously.

Pauline laughed. 'He'd never hurt me. He hasn't had enough exercise lately and I'm hoping to take him for a gallop later on.'

Anthony looked at the slight figure, more like a boy than a girl in her worn jodhpurs and yellow T-shirt, standing so fearlessly beside the big horse. Pegasus was all of sixteen hands.

'Do you mean to say you ride that brute?'

'Of course, and he's not a brute, but strangers make him nervous.'

She came out of the box and closed the door, while George gave an audible sigh of relief. She looked curiously at her visitors, wondering what had brought them. It was too early for a social call and George should have been busy in his garage. She noticed that he was looking sheepish, while

Anthony was looking about him with a speculative eye, as if . . . suspicion awoke in her. She had seen that expression all too often of late. One of the most trying features of waiting for the auction was the would-be purchasers who came to look over the property. She loathed these intrusions and usually managed to absent herself, leaving them to be dealt with by her aunt, who politely showed them round. Marion Thorne had not the same feeling for the place as had her young charges. She was not altogether sorry to be leaving it, since now that she had grown elderly the amenities of town life were becoming more and more attractive, also she had had more than her fill of dealing with the tempestuous Herald temperament and was looking forward to the calmer companionship of her old friend.

George saw that an explanation was necessary, but was unwilling to give it. He cleared his throat.

' I brought Anthony along to . . . er . . . have a look round,' he said nervously.

Pauline's eyes sparkled irefully. ' Since Three Chimneys is up for sale I suppose you regard it as a free entertainment,' she said bitterly.

' Hardly that,' Anthony came to his perspiring friend's rescue. ' The fact is, Miss Herald, I'm thinking of making a bid for the property.'

So she had been right, he was another of her enemies ! She threw a reproachful look at George, the traitor, who had brought his friend down to buy her home.

Meanwhile Anthony was going on unperturbed, ' I'm looking for a house in the country and I was sent the particulars of this place. It seems to be just what I want—quiet, with plenty of grounds, a place I can come to at weekends and holidays, and where eventually I shall retire. This isn't too far from Town and yet it's undeveloped country . . . '

' Oh, it's undeveloped,' she cut it, ' in fact we're practically uncivilized round here. As for the house, no doubt the agent's particulars made it sound delightful, but it's terribly dilapidated. You'd need a fortune to put it in order, and as for drains, I don't think there are any, the sewage just runs into the river . . . '

' Lina ! ' George expostulated.

She became silent and turned away to conceal her trembling lips.

Anthony said coolly, ' Perhaps you'll allow me to judge of all this for myself.'

' Certainly, but I wanted to save you wasting your time.' She had regained her self-control. ' Do you really want to see over it ? '

He stared down into her defiant grey eyes, noticing how long and dark were her eyelashes. Irrelevantly he thought that properly dressed and groomed this little termagant would be remarkably easy on the eye.

' If I may.'

' Oh, well, come on.'

A diversion was caused by the arrival of Duchess, who hearing voices came loping into the yard, barking loudly. Recognizing George, she rushed at him, leaping round him, wagging her plumed tail. They were old friends. Sighting the stranger, she stiffened and her hackles rose.

' Friend, Duch,' George said, stooping to pat her.

Cautiously the dog approached Anthony, who held out a hand, which she sniffed suspiciously, then the tail began to wag, and she licked his fingers.

' Well, she's accepted you,' George said with

relief.

Anthony was stroking Duchess's head. ' She's a lovely dog.'

' She's a soppy old fool,' Pauline said ungraciously, put out by the dog's attitude to Anthony. ' If you want to see the place come on, I haven't got all day to waste.'

George gave his friend an apologetic glance, to which Anthony responded with the sketch of a shrug. Pauline led the way across the paved yard and up a short flight of steps, on to a path which ran upwards, skirting the walled garden. Duchess went with them, walking sedately between the two men. The path was bordered with straggling plants, struggling to exist among the weeds; pansies, pinks, sweet williams, marigolds and double daisies being among the old-fashioned flowers. At the head of the sloping path stood a cherry tree, which was lovely with blossom in the spring, but now looked tired and wilted. On the ground beneath it the residue of its crop lay rotting, and as they approached they saw half a dozen Red Admirals, living mosaics of red, black, white and brown, settled on the debris.

' Butterflies ! ' Anthony exclaimed with delight, ' how beautiful ! '

' They're becoming rare,' Pauline said sadly, ' victims of poison spray.'

In the rose garden, the grass had been roughly cut, and the unpruned trees were suffering from neglect, but they were still in bloom, and masses of Dorothy Perkins' and American Pillar ran riot, their supporting arches collapsing under their weight. A trellis covered with honeysuckle filled the air with sweetness.

' Might be the wreck of the Hesperus,' Pauline described it disparagingly, ' Michael cut the grass,

28

but otherwise it hasn't been touched for years.'

'But it's very lovely,' Anthony said softly, 'and full of possibilities.'

'Expensive ones?' Pauline suggested, as they crossed the levelled rose garden to another flight of steps between a row of tall cypresses, once clipped, but now unruly, which separated it from the tennis court, the turf of which no longer looked like turf.

'We had quite a good hay crop off this,' Pauline informed him. 'It would have to be re-sown or re-turfed to be fit for use, and seed or turves cost the earth.'

George could have shaken her.

She stood on the edge of it, pointing to where a rockery and another flight of steps divided it from the paddock beyond.

'Those trees in the distance mark the end of the property,' she swept her hand towards the right to where ripening pears and apples could be seen over a hedge, 'and that's the orchard, it runs up from behind the stables. The trees all need spraying and pruning. You'd need an army of gardeners to put this place in order.'

Anthony made no rejoinder. In the silence that fell between them, the humming of bees was clearly audible; he turned about; through the gap in the cypresses he could see the roof of the house and beyond it the road running up the rise through Mullings to a blue distance of trees and fields. A heron risen from the river flapped lazily over the house, and somewhere, far overhead, a lark was singing—a peaceful, pastoral scene, rural England at its best. Pauline turned abruptly and began to walk back along the way they had come, and in silence the two men and the dog followed her. At the bottom of the last steps leading down into the yard, she stopped.

'Do you want to see any more, Mr Marsh?'

'Yes, I'd like to see the house.'

She stiffened. 'I suppose you've got an order to view?'

'Oh, really, Lina!' George groaned.

Anthony thrust his hands into his pockets and regarded her quizzically.

'Why don't you want me to buy this place, Miss Herald? Someone's going to, you know.'

She knew that was only too true, knew also that she was behaving childishly. It could make no difference to her exile who bought Three Chimneys, but the thought of this elegant man of the world possessing her home was repugnant to her. He looked as though he might have the means to put it in order, to groom it and trim it until it was as elegant and immaculate as he was himself, turning it into a rich man's plaything, and she loved its shabbiness and the wild untrammelled growth of the grounds as part of its character. She had vaguely hoped that the new owners would be another family, who would love it and leave it unchanged, though this hope was a faint one, since such people did not often have the wherewithal. She rubbed her eyes with one slim brown hand—tears were always near the surface during these difficult days— and managed a faint smile.

'I'm sorry,' she said. 'Frankly I hate the thought of anyone buying Three Chimneys, but that's unreasonable, I know, and you and George did rather catch me on the wrong foot.'

'Under a bundle of hay?' his smile answered hers. 'George should have given you fair warning that we were coming. Won't you forgive us and show us the house?'

'Oh, very well,' she said ungraciously.

She forbore to point out any further disadvantages, as they went through the front rooms, into which the sunlight filtered through the vine leaves, where clusters of small purple grapes were hanging. In the kitchen they came upon Lynette and Aunt Marion busy with their morning chores. After the introductions were performed, there was still the upstairs to examine, and Aunt Marion told them to come down for coffee in the 'drawing room' when they had finished their inspection. This completed, they returned to the room mentioned: the house was L-shaped, and the drawing room ran along the whole side of the house into the L, having in addition to the glass door and windows on to the verandah, a big bay overlooking the walled garden to the right of the house.

Anthony viewed the long, low room, with its wide, open hearth, and drew a long breath.

'I don't wonder you love this place,' he said to Pauline. 'I could love it too.'

To Pauline this was the worst thing he could have said. That he, this alien, should dare to link himself with her in love for her birthplace, which he was seeing for the first time, seemed to her to be the height of presumption. She said sharply, 'It all looks very pretty in the summer, but it's a bit grim in the winter.'

'It's a long time since I saw real snow in England,' he said. 'In London it becomes dirty slush almost as soon as it's fallen.'

'We don't usually have much snow,' Pauline told him, 'but we do have lots of mud.'

'I daresay I could put up with even that.' His eyes surveyed her with a mocking glint, but she refused to meet his glance, lowering her thick lashes

31

over her own eyes. She was deciding that she had never met anyone whom she disliked as much as Anthony Marsh; the ' in England ' had not escaped her. No doubt he was familiar with Switzerland, and the playgrounds of Europe. He was a playboy, a layabout, and as such she despised him with all her heart. The arrival of Aunt Marion with the coffee pot cut short her reflections and Anthony's attempts to propitiate her. Michael was out hacking with a couple of local girls—the money for lessons and Aunt Marion's slender means was all they had to live upon during the weeks of waiting. Lynette handed round cups and biscuits very prettily, and was busy appraising the visitor. He was utterly different from anyone she had ever seen before. Most of the young men of her acquaintance were bucolic types, whose friendly banter caused her to shrink from them in terror. When she brought Anthony his cup and he demurred, saying he should be waiting upon her, her shy disclaimer was accompanied by a vivid blush. She thought he was like the hero of one of her favourite romances, Sir Lancelot du Lac or Rhett Butler in *Gone with the Wind*. She wondered if he were married and if he would bring his wife to live at Three Chimneys if he bought the place. She hoped he would make some comment which would reveal either his intentions, or his status, but the conversation never went beyond what is termed ' small talk ', the weather, the state of the roads, the increasing cost of living.

Though that, Pauline thought bitterly, eyeing Anthony's clothes and remembering Anthony's car, won't cause him any inconvenience.

She noticed that he seemed to be looking for something in the downstairs rooms, and after a

further glance round the long room, he said wonderingly,

'Can it be that you don't have a television ? '

Aunt Marion laughed, ' No, we've never had one,
my nephew always declared it was a time-waster.'

' He only wanted to see the Horse of the Year Show
or the racing, and he said it wasn't worth paying
for one just for that,' Lynette informed him, and
blushed again at her own temerity.

' Actually we did have one for three months,'
Pauline remarked, and forbore to add that it had
been removed because the instalments had not been
paid.

George coughed. ' When there's anything special
on, they have a free invitation to come and watch
on my set.' He glanced apologetically at his friend,
and Pauline sensed an undercurrent, especially when
Anthony said ruefully, ' I suppose it isn't as important as we like to think it is,' but neither of them
offered an explanation. Soon afterwards, as they
rose to go, Lynette ventured to say shyly:

' I do hope you decide to buy Three Chimneys,
Mr Marsh. I'd like to think of you here when
we've gone.'

' That's very sweet of you,' Anthony told her,
while Pauline frowned. It was obvious to her
that Lynette had fallen heavily for the stranger.
' And very forgiving,' he added with a sly glance
at the elder sister. Pauline averted her head,
pretending not to have heard him.

As George and Anthony reached the front gate,
they had walked down from the garage, they met
Michael bringing home his two pupils. They stood
aside as the little cavalcade went passed them,
Michael saluting them with his crop. Anthony

was looking thoughtful.

' So you think this riding school is a paying proposition ? ' he asked.

' I'm sure it could be,' George said emphatically, having his own axe to grind, ' but Lina and Mike need someone to take them in hand. They haven't much idea of business—not their fault, their dad was like that, but they could be taught.' He looked anxiously at his friend, but Anthony did not rise.

' Poor kids,' was all he said.

Anthony Marsh's visit could not fail to arouse much speculation in Mullings. He had spent two nights with George, and he was from the great sprawling city of London, which was still to the older inhabitants as remote as outer space. When it was reported that he had visited Three Chimneys anticipation ran high. The man appeared to have money, and a wealthy owner of that property would benefit all and sundry. John Herald with his borrowings and insolvency had been more of a liability than an asset to his neighbours. Then the place had been allowed to run down, and there had been much head-shaking over its fate, but if it could attract a solid purchaser from London there was still hope for it. The two younger Heralds were no less curious about him than their neighbours, but while they made no secret of their interest, Pauline pretended indifference. But when, on the evening following his friend's visit, George appeared on the verandah, tapping on the window for admittance, her eyes eagerly searched the shadowed dusk behind him for the tall figure which had already become familiar, and she experienced a stab of relief when she discovered that he was alone; at least she told herself it was relief, but it was curiously akin to disappointment. That Michael and Lynette were disappointed was obvious. George was waving a motor magazine.

'Something in here I thought might interest Mike,' he said to excuse his late call. Michael took the paper indifferently. Beyond registering at the Labour Exchange he had done nothing towards finding a job, being convinced that when it came to the crunch, Pauline would accept George's hand.

'Where's Mr Marsh?' he asked.

Pauline was grateful to him for asking the question that she was too proud to put for herself.

'Oh, Ant's gone back to London,' George said casually. 'Couldn't stay any longer. He's got a job, you know.'

Pauline raised her fine brows. 'You don't mean to tell me Mr Marsh works for a living?'

'But of course.' George looked bewildered by the scorn in her voice. 'Don't we all?'

'*We* do,' she emphasized the pronoun, 'or at least we try to,' she sighed, knowing how unsuccessful their efforts had been, 'but I thought he was a playboy.'

'He must have a darned good job if he can afford to buy Three Chimneys,' Michael said bluntly, 'what's he do?'

George became vague. 'Well . . . er . . . I'm never quite sure, some sort of executive position.'

'You're being impertinent, Mike,' Aunt Marion said repressively.

'Oh, I didn't mean to be nosey,' Michael said airily. 'I'd no idea he was a mystery man. Has he robbed a bank or some such?'

'Don't be absurd,' Pauline reproved him. 'Mr Marsh's affairs are of no interest to us—anyway, I'm sure he hasn't robbed a bank, he wouldn't have the guts.'

Lynette looked reproachfully at her sister.
'Lina's got her knife into him,' she complained.
'I can't think why, he seemed so nice.'

'Because he's interested in Three Chimneys,'
George explained. 'She did her darnedest to crab
the place when she showed him round. If she goes
on like that, you won't get a bid, and your debts'll
never be settled.'

'Oh, Lina, how could you!' Lynette stared at
Pauline wide-eyed.

Pauline was leafing through George's magazine.
'Must we keep on discussing Mr Marsh?' she asked.
'I don't suppose we'll ever see him again, and we've
many more important things to think about.'

She could not altogether explain her antipathy
to Anthony Marsh. She told herself that it was
because he was smarmy and supercilious, though in
actual fact he had been neither. The truth was
much more fundamental. During her short life,
she had lorded it over George and the local swains,
and wheedled her father into getting most of what
she wanted. She sensed that in Anthony she had
met a man who would be impervious to wiles, and
whose will was stronger than her own. He disconcerted her, and she hoped that she had spoken
the truth when she had said they would not be
seeing him again.

Some days later Mr Smithers came to see them.
He was their family solicitor, a small, elderly man,
as dried-up and leathery as his own briefcase.
Pauline, who was in the office, watched him coming
up the drive to the house with a feeling of foreboding; he would be for ever connected in her mind
with the awful day upon which he had had to explain

their position to them. Coming directly after her father's accident, the double shock had all but shattered her. She wondered apprehensively what further catastrophe he had come to announce.

As it happened the family were in the house, and were quickly assembled when Mr Smithers told her that he wished to speak to them all. The gathering had all the sinister overtones of the previous occasion, and looking at their anxious young faces, the solicitor managed a tight-lipped smile which was meant to be reassuring.

'This time I have some good news for you,' he told them.

Michael sprang up eagerly. 'You mean there's been a mistake? We shan't have to be sold up after all?'

Pauline clasped her hands and her heart quickened as new hope was born, but surely such news would be too good to be true.

It was not true.

'There won't have to be an auction,' Mr Smithers went on. 'The whole place has been sold, lock, stock and barrel by private treaty.'

'Oh!' Pauline sighed, as disappointment surged through her, and Michael subsided. Only Lynette continued to look eagerly at Mr Smithers.

'Who's bought it?' she asked.

Pauline knew. 'Mr Marsh, of course,' she said dully.

'It's a comfort in one way,' Aunt Marion said placidly. 'I disliked the idea of all our things being auctioned piecemeal. So degrading.'

A new thought occurred to Pauline. 'Surely he isn't buying the horses?' she asked anxiously. 'He didn't strike me as being horse-minded.'

Mr Smithers cleared his throat and adjusted his

glasses.

'Quite so,' he murmured, 'that's where my good news comes in. He wishes to continue with the riding school and he has asked me to make a proposition to you.'

Pauline sprang to her feet. 'I don't want to hear any proposition from Mr Marsh,' she cried angrily. She was not surprised, as all along some sixth sense had warned her that Anthony would suggest some scheme that would humiliate her and she was determined that nothing would persuade her to have any dealings with him.

'Lina, sit down,' Aunt Marion said sharply, she turned apologetically to the solicitor. 'Please excuse my niece, Mr Smithers, she's a little overwrought. What does Mr Marsh propose?'

Mr Smithers glanced apprehensively at Pauline's flushed face. The Heralds were, he well knew, both passionate and headstrong. He had not approved of Mr Marsh's quixotic suggestion and thought that gentleman had little idea of what he was rashly undertaking, but it was his duty to his young clients in their own interests to advise them to accept.

'Mr Marsh,' he began pompously, 'is a bachelor at present. (What does he mean by that, Pauline wondered; is there a lady in the offing?) He is looking for a country estate in which to invest a legacy which he has recently inherited.' He paused.

'How dull,' Michael the irrepressible exclaimed. 'We were sure he'd robbed a bank.'

Mr Smithers frowned at him, annoyed by his levity. 'In that he is wise,' he went on, raising his voice slightly. 'Real estate is a good investment and likely to increase in value. Three Chimneys appeals to him for several reasons,' he rustled the papers he was holding. Mr Smithers always seemed to be holding papers, as if they gave him confidence. No doubt the present ones set forth Anthony's reasons for wanting to invest in Three Chimneys. He went on, ' As yet, he cannot live here himself, so he has suggested that you stay on as tenants.'

' That's fine,' Michael exclaimed, ' but where's the rent coming from ? '

' You will pay no rent,' he was told, ' and you will only occupy part of the house. Mr Marsh requires the best rooms for his own use when he comes down at the weekend or for a holiday. To you, ma'am,' he turned to Aunt Marion, ' he offers the position of housekeeper, since he will require meals and service when he is in residence, for this he will pay you a quite generous salary. Miss and Mr Herald,' he glanced nervously at Pauline's stony face, ' are to run the riding school as instructors, with a small salary and . . . er . . . a share of the profits, if any,' he emphasized the last two words, he had his own opinion of the merits of the riding school, ' you will have to keep careful accounts,' he looked sternly at Pauline, ' to discover if the venture really does pay. You will have no objection to doing that ? '

Michael laughed, ' Lina can't add two and two without making five.'

Pauline felt as if she were choking. It was obvious to her that Anthony believed that she was inefficient and wanted to show her up. He thought she was playing with her riding school and this was how he meant to bring it home to her.

Mr Smithers was again frowning at Michael.

' This offer is a serious one, Mr Herald,' he said sharply.

' I think it's wonderful,' Lynette exclaimed, her

eyes shining. 'So very generous—only what can I do?'

Mr Smithers' face relaxed and he smiled at her eagerness.

'Mr Marsh hopes that you will continue to make Three Chimneys your home,' he told her.

'I knew he was good and kind,' Lynette cried enthusiastically, 'he understood how unhappy we all were, and now we needn't leave home and you'll still have the horses, Lina. How can we thank him enough?'

Pauline clenched her hands. Lynette was still a child, she believed in fairy godmothers, or in this case, godfather, but she herself was old enough to know nobody did anything for nothing. She could not work for this man, whom she despised as a layabout and a cissy, nor could she bear to see him master of all that she had loved and cherished, while he exposed all her inadequacies and mocked them. She would not bear it, she would rather earn her living doing the lowest menial work than submit to it. Controlling her anger, she said in what she hoped was a sarcastic voice:

'And for how long does this delectable arrangement continue? Until he gets married?'

Mr Smithers rustled his papers and coughed. 'Mr Marsh did not confide his matrimonial intentions to me,' he said drily. 'No doubt you will receive proper notice of any change of plan. I gather the arrangement will be more or less provisional,' he looked severely at Pauline and Michael. 'You will be on probation as it were.'

'Quite,' Pauline returned his look. 'He'd make an excellent probation officer.'

Mr Smithers sighed with exasperation. 'Miss Herald, I advise you to accept this offer, even if only on a temporary basis, because whatever happens, your position can't be worse than it is now.'

' I for one shall be only too thankful to accept this most generous offer,' Aunt Marion announced. ' The arrangements I was making can be postponed indefinitely. I'm quite ready to stay on here until the children have had time to find their feet, and if it doesn't work out, we shall at least have had a breathing space.'

She gave a little sigh, as she saw her dream of a cosy flat in Town vanishing over the horizon, while she made up her mind to do her best for a new and unpredictable employer. She had been more worried about Michael and Pauline than she had cared to admit, but she did not expect any recognition of her unselfishness. The young people had always taken her for granted and did not realize what she was sacrificing for them.

' I'm all for it too,' Michael said. ' It'll do until I can find an opening with a motor firm.'

They all looked at Pauline. She faced them with a brilliant spot of colour on either cheek, her grey eyes sparkling. ' I couldn't dream of accepting,' she said. ' It . . . it's charity. The riding school's no good, I'm no good, Mike's no good . . .'

' Oh, come off it, Sis,' Michael interrupted, ' speak for yourself ! '

' But I *am* an efficient housekeeper,' Aunt Marion interposed calmly, ' which I rather think is Mr Marsh's greatest need.' She turned to Mr Smithers. ' You can tell him we are all only too glad to accept his very generous terms, and we'll endeavour to do our best to give satisfaction—I believe that's the correct phrase ? ' she smiled a little wanly. ' And now, Mr Smithers, I'm sure you're longing for a cup of tea. Come into the drawing room and rest while I make you one.'

She led the solicitor through into the long room, which she was deciding would be one of those Anthony would require for his private use. As the door closed behind them, Michael turned on his sister.

'What's the big idea?' he demanded. 'Even if we aren't any good, it'll take Mr Marsh some time to find us out. Don't you see this arrangement is a positive godsend for us? You won't marry George, and now you want to turn down this excellent offer out of some silly fancy, pride or pique. You might at least think of Lynette and me.'

'I'm not stopping you from accepting,' Pauline flashed at him, 'but I won't stay under his roof, and don't forget it *is* his roof!'

'Oh, please, Lina,' Lynette was half crying, 'don't go away. It'll spoil everything—I was so delighted that we'd still all be together. Why must you go? Surely you can't bear to leave Pegasus?'

Pegasus? She had forgotten Pegasus. Once, it seemed a century ago, she had had vague dreams for his future. She would train him to be a show jumper, and perhaps be a second Marion Coakes, and her father had encouraged her ambitions, though she had never got beyond the local horse shows. Anthony would have no sympathy with such aspirations. Pegasus would have to be tamed into an economic proposition. She walked to the window and leaned her head against the pane, glad of its coolness against her hot forehead. Outside the sun shone indifferently on the dahlias coming into flower in the neglected borders, and the tender green fronds of the weeping willow.

'I don't honestly believe this arrangement would work,' she said dully. 'Aunt Marion's all right, of course, but we're all wrong.'

'You might at least try it,' Michael urged, 'but of course if you're determined to fail right from the start, you won't give it a chance.'

'I've told you you can go ahead,' she repeated, 'but I'm not staying to be bullied and driven by that ... that ...' She tried to think of a sufficiently unpleasant word to describe Anthony.

'I'm sure he won't bully you,' Lynette insisted in her soft voice. 'You make him sound like a slave-driver.'

'How do you know he isn't?' She swung round to face her sister. 'You're creating a romantic image of him to fall for, which isn't the real him at all.'

Michael said, 'If you back out, he may call the whole thing off. I can't manage the school by myself, and I've a hunch you're one of the attractions.'

Her eyes widened, behind her the sunlight made a burnished halo of her hair, with the angry colour staining the delicate tan of her cheeks, she looked more than pretty.

'Me?' she gasped. 'I haven't even been pleasant to him.'

Michael grinned. 'But you're nice to look at,' he said, 'and he may prefer 'em hard to get. No doubt he's bored with the come-hither types and would like to do a bit of chasing himself for a change.'

'Mike, you're abominable!' She was furious.

Lynette was looking pensive. 'It would be lovely if you and he fell in love.'

'And he's a much better catch than poor old

43

George,' added Michael, who was not above baiting his sister when occasion offered. 'Play your cards right and you'll get Three Chimneys offered to you on a plate.'

Pauline's cheeks flamed scarlet. 'That's not funny,' she said fiercely. 'Remember he's years older than we are, and sophisticated. Perhaps he fancies sweet simplicity and all the ye olde stuff for a change, but it's my guess that the novelty will soon wear off. Before that happens I hope I'll have found a job on the other side of England.'

She opened the catch of the door and stepped out into the verandah, banging it behind her. Lynette and Michael looked at each other.

'Oh dear,' Lynette wailed, 'now you've done it, Mike. She won't stay.'

'Oh yes, she will,' Michael was unperturbed. 'You see, she'll come round. Meanwhile, I think I'd better invest in a ready reckoner.'

Pauline went straight to the stables and flung a saddle across Pegasus. She could not remember whether anyone was coming for a lesson, and she did not care, she felt she had to get away from the house, Mr Smithers and his propositions, and Mike's insinuations. She rode up the lane, to where a grass ride led off to a stretch of heathland, and let Pegasus have his head. The gallop relieved her pent-up feelings, and when at length he slowed to a trot and finally a walk, she began to consider Anthony's offer seriously. She could not understand how any business man—and he must be a good business man, if he held, as George had told them, an executive position—could believe that the riding school was a sound financial proposition. She suspected—correctly—that George had exaggerated its possibilities, yet she well knew that other people had made a success out of similar ventures. That they had not done so must be, she admitted honestly, due to their own happy-go-lucky methods and ignorance. Mr Marsh would correct all that, and she winced at the prospect. She could not rid herself of the suspicion that he deliberately wanted to humiliate her by showing up her incompetence. She had been, if not actually rude, by no means pleasant to him, and he was the sort of man who expected adulation from women, and usually got it. She feared that if she accepted the position, he would take a malicious delight in exposing her inefficiency and calling her to account for her lapses. But Michael could not cope with the school without her, and he and Lynette were eager to stay on in their old home, while the alternatives for herself were not attractive. She could only expect to get an ill-paid drudgery of a job, or marry George. She would be wiser to give the thing a trial, and if at the end of it she and Michael were sacked for their inadequacies, they would be in no worse position than they were now, and they would have a breathing space to look around, as their aunt had said. Poor Aunt Marion, her position would not be an enviable one, she was doing it for their sake and if she could humble herself to accept a subordinate position, she, Pauline, could do likewise. Then again, need the venture be a failure ? If she put her back into it, worked as she had never worked before, accepted all the corrections and humiliations which she foresaw meekly, could she not manage to make a go of it ? If her prospective employer had been anyone except Anthony Marsh, she would not hesitate, but she loathed the idea of having to submit to his authority, not realizing that subconsciously she wanted to impress him and doubted her ability to do so. As for Michael's absurd suggestions about the personal aspect, and she still felt hot all over when she recalled them, of course he had been only teasing her, and he would have to learn to control his tongue. The last person for whom she could imagine herself cherishing tender feelings was Anthony, and she had laid herself out to make him dislike her, which he probably did. The relationship between them would be that of master and servant, any other idea was preposterous, and only a romantic little fool like Lynette would entertain it. She remembered with relief that he would only appear for the odd weekend and occasional holidays, and the weekends were always her busiest time, so that their actual contacts would be few and far between.

She turned Pegasus' head homewards and he broke into a canter, eager for his oats and stable.

The horses too needed her, their fate hung on her decision. Well, she had made it; she must learn to be cool and detached, to accept reprimands humbly and obey her employer's orders unquestioningly. It would not be easy, but she would make herself do it, and perhaps as a reward the riding school would begin to flourish.

CHAPTER III

Pauline contrived to be absent when Anthony Marsh next visited the house, but she learned afterwards that he had had a long talk with Aunt Marion about his plans. The drawing room was to be redecorated and furnished for his exclusive use, together with the two bedrooms in the L, one of which was to be turned into an additional bathroom. A gardener was to be employed as soon as the purchase was completed, when work would start on the alterations. Anthony left a set of books for Pauline's use, which she viewed with considerable apprehension.

'It's all quite simple,' Michael said cheerfully, opening the cash-book. ' You put on one side all the money you receive and on the other what you pay out.'

'I know all that,' Pauline said irritably, 'I'm not a moron, but I've also got to estimate the amount of grub each beast eats in a year, and how many times he's used—poor Peg is going to show up badly, nobody can ride him except you and me.'

' Then you'll have to use your wiles to persuade Mr Marsh to keep him.'

' Oh, for heaven's sake, Mike, don't let's have any more of that nonsense ! '

' Don't bicker, you two,' Aunt Marion admonished them. ' Remember it's up to both of you to give Mr Marsh loyal and honest service since he's been so generous.'

Pauline's dark brows drew together ominously. ' If anyone mentions Mr Marsh's generosity again, I'll be sick ! ' she interrupted. ' You make us sound like paupers he's rescued from destitution.'

'And that,' Michael said airily, 'is about what we are.'

Nonetheless, Pauline stuck to her determination to do her best in her new role. Her employer should have no cause to complain of her. The stable work, the care of the string of eight horses and ponies, presented no difficulties, she had done it for most of her life, nor was she lacking in patience with her pupils, some of whom obviously would never make horsewomen—they were mostly girls—but were learning because they wanted to be ' with it', but paper work was unfamiliar ground. The fodder they had to purchase seemed to cost alarming amounts now that she had to keep a careful check of her spendings—in her father's day the stuff was delivered usually on credit with no regard to expense—and she had to chase her brother to make sure that he had handed over the fees he had collected. Once a week she went by bus to Melford to bank the takings, not daring to entrust him with this errand. But try as she would, the entries in her large sprawling handwriting never seemed to quite tally with the actual cash in hand.

August passed into September, and completion was duly effected. Anthony rang up to say that he would be coming down on the next Saturday to take possession of his domain. Saturday brought a sunny morning, with a heavy dew on the grass, and the early morning mist still lingering over the distances like a pearly veil. There was no wind, and the trees were still and heavy with the growth of foliage they would soon discard. The fields where the corn had been carried showed white stubble, except where they had been scored with black streaks, where the straw had been burned off. The last flowers of summer's pageant blazed in every garden, golden rod, michaelmas daisies, coreopsis, and the brilliant hues of dahlias. The countryside was smiling and gay to greet the new-comer.

Aunt Marion baked and roasted, swept and cleaned, assisted by Lynette, who put flowers out of the garden in Anthony's rooms. Pauline glanced dismally at her smudged account books, closed them with a bang, and went to the more congenial task of grooming her horses. As she passed through the kitchen, she noticed that her aunt had put on a speckless nylon overall over her neat blouse and skirt, and Lynette was wearing her one good dress, a printed silk. Her sister glanced disparagingly at Pauline's jodhpurs and yellow T-shirt, which was not particularly clean.

' Aren't you going to change ? ' she asked timidly. ' Michael's put on a clean shirt and spruced himself up.'

Pauline scowled. ' No, why should I ? Saturday's a busy day and at least Mr Marsh can see I'm working.' She glanced scornfully at Lynette's frock and the younger girl coloured guiltily.

' I . . . I wanted to look nice. First impressions are important, don't you think ? '

' He's already had those,' Pauline pointed out, ' and I'm not going to doll myself up for him.'

He drove the Jaguar straight up into the stable yard. Michael had been watching ready to open the gate for him. Pauline heard its approach and moved out of sight from the open stable door. She heard also the car door slam and his voice as he spoke to Michael, and was struck afresh with what a beautiful enunciation he had. Even George mangled the English language upon occasion. She vigorously brushed the coat of the bay mare that stood between her and the door, aware that her heart was beating unusually fast, and her face had flushed, but she did not relax until she was sure that the men had gone into the house, then she went to the open door in search of cooler air to soothe her hot cheeks.

Michael came into the yard, calling: 'Hi, Lina, he wants to see you.'

'I can't come now,' she turned back to saddle the mare. 'You know the Draytons are due at eleven and it's five to now—Oh, here they are!'

A Ford convertible drove into the yard, and halted by the Jaguar. From it a bevy of youngsters descended in immaculate hacking clothes. They shouted for attention.

'Surely they can wait while you say how do you do,' Michael whispered to her.

'No, they can't,' she snapped. 'They're my best customers. Give me a hand with the tack.'

In the ensuing mêlée while they mounted six riders on six horses, Pauline had only one thought, to get her convoy under way before Anthony came in search of her. With the youngest member of the party, a child of ten on a leading rein, she mounted the bay mare—she never rode Pegasus when escorting tyros—and marshalled the party out of the side gate, which Michael opened for them, with a sigh of relief. She had escaped without encountering him.

But she had to come back. When, after an hour of encouraging the more timid and restraining the too enthusiastic, the party returned to the yard, she was again in a state of agitation, and involuntarily her eyes raked garden and yard for a sight of him. She was regretting the impulse that had

50

urged her to flee; it would have been more sensible to get the first meeting over, as her brother had suggested, before she went out. Now the ordeal still lay before her. Michael should have been there to help her unsaddle, but he was not. With the aid of the more experienced students, she stabled all the animals and rubbed them down. The Draytons departed in their convertible, after the usual business of booking their next lesson and paying for the one just over. Pauline thrust the banknotes into her pocket, hoping she would remember who had paid what, and made a mental note of dates and times, then as she turned towards the house, a scooter came round the corner into the yard ridden by two plain young women, the Misses Fraser, smart in jodhpurs and velvet caps—Michael's pupils. He had not mentioned that they were coming, and she suspected that he had forgotten all about them. She hurried into the house in search of him, and Aunt Marion said he was in the office; this, the third room in front of the house, was much smaller than the other two, and had always been her father's sanctum. It contained two worn leather-covered armchairs, a roll-topped desk, a small table, and sporting prints on the walls. She threw open the door, and stopped short, staring with increasing anger at what she saw. The desk, her desk now, was open and several bottles had been placed upon it, Anthony and Michael were sprawled in the armchairs in front of a small fire burning in the grate, each with a tumbler at his elbow in a haze of blue cigarette smoke. Duchess, the traitress, had her head on Anthony's knee, and was gazing up at him soppy-eyed, but the crowning offence in Pauline's eyes was that her account books were open on the men's knees and both of them were laughing merrily, apparently at her efforts.

Ignoring Anthony, she spoke to Michael. 'The Miss Frasers are in the yard. You never said they were coming, and all the horses have been out except Bonny and Pegasus.'

'Oh, help, I'd forgotten all about them,' Michael rose reluctantly to his feet, letting the precious cash-book slide to the floor.

'Mike!' her voice was full of reproach. She had so wanted to appear efficient and everything seemed to be working against her. 'You'll have to take Dinah, she's so lazy she's still fairly fresh.'

'They don't like me to ride Pegasus,' Michael told her. 'He scares them when he prances. Can't we put them off?'

'No, that wouldn't be fair, they've come a long way. You'll just have to keep Peg in order. Do hurry, Mike, they're waiting.' She glanced at Anthony. 'Whatever will Mr Marsh think of us?' He was regarding her with amusement, and she became aware that she was flushed and dishevelled. She groped in her pocket for her handkerchief, which was not there, only the notes and coins, which scattered all over the floor.

'Paid cash, did they?' Michael retrieved a couple of notes. 'Nice to see so much lolly, but you might treat it more respectfully.'

'Go along, Mike,' she was crimson with mortification.

He strolled to the door. 'Cheer up, Sis,' he said cheerfully. 'Mr Marsh has been studying your industrious book-keeping, and he's much impressed.' He went out whistling, closing the door behind him. She was about to follow him, feeling she could bear no more, when Anthony's voice recalled her.

'Do sit down, Miss Herald, I'd like to talk to you.'

'Can't it wait?' she flung at him, near to tears. 'I want to have a bath.'

'No, I can't wait, your bath will have to do that. Please sit down.' His voice was pleasant but firm. He had collected the money she had scattered and was placing it carefully on the desk. She whirled round to face him, all her resolutions forgotten.

'I know what you're going to say—we're no good, we're hopelessly inefficient. I always said it wouldn't work, and you'd much better get rid of us before we ruin you!'

'My dear girl, don't be so childish,' he said calmly.

She turned back to the door, blindly fumbling for the handle, aware that the angry tears were falling down her cheeks.

'I'm not your dear girl, I don't want to hear what you've got to say. I'm going . . .'

His hand gripped her elbow urgently, and he propelled her towards the chair.

'Do as I say.'

Pauline subsided into it perforce, brushing her hand across her wet eyes. She heard the sound of liquid being poured into a glass.

'Drink this, and wipe your face.'

He was holding out a tumbler and a clean white handkerchief.

'I . . . I don't want it.' She would like to have thrown it into his face.

'Take it,' he insisted.

She grabbed the handkerchief which she vaguely noticed smelled of lavender and buried her face in it; through its folds she heard that hateful insistent voice. 'Now your drink.'

Unwillingly she took the tumbler and drank. It was soda water with a dash of spirits, and it warmed and soothed her. Duchess came to her and put an insinuating paw on her knee. She began to stroke the dog's head while she tried to regain her self-control. She looked up and met Anthony's eyes fixed upon her, and saw with surprise they were not really dark, but a clear hazel, greeny grey with amber lights. Under their intent gaze she hastily dropped her own.

'Come' he said kindly, 'I'm sure you've too much spirit to give in at the first fence. I see you've been working very hard, though perhaps not very accurately,' he picked up the cash-book, 'also you ought to keep an engagement book, then little contretemps like the one that has just occurred wouldn't happen.'

She remembered guiltily that she had not written down the Draytons' next appearance—was it on Tuesday or Wednesday?—and nodded miserably.

For the next hour he went over her books with her, explaining and suggesting. Her corn bills were very high, could she not find a cheaper source of supply? Michael had told him that she had plenty of travellers calling upon her. He thought Coopers offered better terms than Brown, her present supplier.

She moved restlessly. 'I don't like their representative, he . . . he gets fresh,' and regretted the admission.

'Then make Michael deal with him, and couldn't you write a little more neatly?'

She swallowed, resisting an impulse to further rebellion, remembering that she must be prepared to accept criticism.

'I . . . I'll try.'

'Good girl! That'll do for today.'

Pauline gently pushed Duchess away and rose to

her feet. She had made a poor start towards keeping her resolutions, and she felt she owed him an apology.

'I'm sorry I made such a scene,' she said humbly, 'and it's awfully good of you to be so patient with me.' She looked at the wet ball of handkerchief which she still clutched. 'I'll get Lynette to wash this out.' She met his eyes squarely. 'I'll do my best to ... er ... give satisfaction.' She remembered Aunt Marion's phrase.

'That's all right,' he said cheerfully. 'I'm hoping I can assist to equip you to face the rat race of life. Lack of discipline and inefficiency won't help you if ever you need to take another position.'

Pauline was chilled by his last words. Childishly she had expected a warmer reception of her apology.

'Now may I go and have my bath?'

'First enter this money and put it in the cash-box.'

Schoolmaster, she thought as she obediently did as she was told.

He looked at her scrawl doubtfully. 'I suppose you can read it?'

'It's undisciplined, like me,' she said shortly, 'but I can read it, and strangely enough, so can Mike.'

She closed the book and went towards the door, where his voice stopped her again.

'After your bath, you might perhaps put on a skirt?'

She stared at him blankly. 'A ... skirt?'

'Yes. Since it's my first day in residence, your aunt has kindly suggested that we all have lunch together, and I prefer to eat with a young lady, not a stable boy.'

'Oh!' The door slammed on her exit, and Anthony's laughter.

While she bathed, she resolved that nothing would make her dress up for Anthony's benefit. Wrapped in an ancient dressing gown, she went to the little back room which had always been hers, since she preferred that her aunt should move into the big front room that had been her father's. If she leaned out of her window, she could see the stables to the right, which was one reason why she liked the room; another was the climbing rose, the blooms of which hung round the sill. She picked up her worn jodhpurs and paused with them in her hand. She had to give another lesson during the afternoon and then there would be the bedding and feeding to do. She could not be continually changing her clothes to please Anthony's whims, and he ought not to expect it. Nevertheless, she dropped the garment and drew aside the curtain concealing the alcove which did duty for a wardrobe. Her collection of dresses was meagre, there had been no money for replenishments, neither had she had much occasion to wear frocks. A green crimplene caught her eye, her most recent acquisition, and slipping out of her dressing gown, she put it on. It was very plain and simply made, but the colour suited her clear skin and showed up the glint of copper in her hair. She combed the latter into a semblance of order and pushed her narrow feet into a pair of cream casuals. She had no long mirror in her room, but the dressing table glass showed a slightly tanned face, wide across the cheekbones, tapering to a pointed chin, big grey eyes surrounded by dark lashes, under well marked brows. She used no make-up, but she looked as fresh and blooming as a spring blossom. A bell rang below stairs announcing that lunch was ready, so that she had no time to repent of her impulse. She must go down wearing the requested skirt and allow Anthony his victory.

He tactfully said nothing, but his eyes showed his approval as she took her place at the table. He was sitting at its head, and with a pang she realized he was in her father's place. Three Chimneys had accepted its new master. Mike was eyeing her with consternation across the table.

'Have you packed up for the day? I can't do everything single-handed.'

'Of course I haven't, but . . . er . . .' she flushed.

Aunt Marion said gently, 'I'm glad you've changed, dear, this little meal is something of an occasion.'

'It is,' Anthony corroborated, 'and as such we're going to celebrate it. I've bought a bottle of wine.'

She noticed then that the table was set with the cut glass wine glasses, one of her father's most cherished possessions, and winced as she remembered that they now belonged to the intruder. Anthony filled her glass, and she looked curiously at the long brown hand that held the bottle, a well-kept hand with carefully manicured nails, and wondered vaguely what he did for a living. Obviously his job paid him well, and equally obviously it did not involve manual work. The conversation veered to, of all unlikely subjects, East Anglian churches, about which Aunt Marion was very well informed.

'We are very proud of our fifteenth-century churches,' she was saying, 'and round here we have some of the finest of the Wool Churches, as they were called, being built from the profits on wool, Tavenham, Melford and Nayland. They are constructed of flint, stone and brick being hard to come by, and the villagers used to collect the flints in baskets off the fields for the builders' use.'

'All erected to the glory of God out of the sweat and toil of the wretched serfs,' Michael said flippantly.

'On the contrary, everyone gave their labour and money willingly and the builders themselves were master craftsmen. In those days the church was the centre of village life, not only for their religious exercises, but it was also their theatre, their recreation hall, sometimes even their court of law. Trading was done in the church porch, feasts celebrated in the nave. They were proud of their church and vied with each other to make theirs the finest. You can imagine the good folk of Tavenham saying to Melford, "Our tower is higher than yours," and Melford returning, "Ah, but our nave is longer." Of course all we have left now is the outer shell, but before they were despoiled they were full of paintings, carvings, gorgeous hangings, gold and jewels.'

'In fact a sight for sore eyes,' her nephew suggested.

'Exactly, an oasis of light and beauty in a rather grim world.'

This conversation Pauline thought must be boring Anthony stiff, but to her surprise, he was looking at her aunt with quite genuine interest.

'One of your shells is at Tavenham, isn't it?' he remarked. 'The tower is a landmark for miles. Will you let me take you there tomorrow?'

Aunt Marion hesitated. 'I usually go to our Parish Church for morning service.'

'Couldn't your devotions be equally well performed at Tavenham?'

'You wouldn't want to wait for the service?'

'Why not?' and in response to her quick look of surprise, 'I'm not entirely a heathen, you know, and it's one way of seeing one's neighbours.

He wants to play the village squire, Pauline thought, but at least it'll give us a lift. Since the demise of the Mini—it had been a write-off—she had been accompanying her aunt to church on a humble bicycle.

Sunday afternoons and evenings were devoted to would-be equestrians, who regarded it as a holiday, but Pauline had always kept the morning hours free for church, so next morning the four of them duly set forth in style in the Jaguar. Anthony was dressed in a well tailored suit, and she thought that he showed up her family's shabbiness, and well knew that the curiosity of the locals would be at fever pitch when he appeared in their company. She began to wish they had refused his escort.

The great tower of Tavenham was indeed a landmark; a hundred and forty-one feet high, it dwarfed the nave behind it, with its huge windows and high clerestory; the buttresses on the tower showed fine examples of flush work, the use of dressed flints to form patterns, a feature of churches of its period. It had been built mainly through the efforts of one Thomas Spring, a clothier, who died a knight, and the Earl of Oxford, to the eternal glory of God.

'It's not a church, it's a young cathedral,' Anthony said, impressed. 'But however did they expect to fill a great place like that?'

'I don't suppose that worried them,' Aunt Marion returned. 'Though in those days everyone went to church, they liked plenty of space for their processions, and the interior wasn't bare like it is now, but filled with chantry chapels, screens, images and candles.'

Inside the September sun poured into the aisles, where the soaring arches of the bays dwarfed the

rather sparse congregation. Pauline contrived to
be the first to enter their row, so that Lynette and
Aunt Marion were between her and Anthony, whose
presence she feared might disturb her devotions.
As she had anticipated there was much rustling and
twisting of heads in their direction to view the
stranger, and by now, most of them would know
who he was, but after a while she forgot her surroundings as she followed the service. The sermon
was not particularly interesting, and she fell into
a half doze. Then it seemed to her that the whole
place had changed. The bare stonework was
covered with tapestry and pictures, candles burned
in pyramids of light before images of saints whose
glittering jewels reflected their light in points of
fire. The carving of the screen was picked out in
gold and brooding above it, illuminated by a row
of lights along the candle beam, was the Rood.
The preacher's voice faded into the drone of plain-
song, as down the aisle came a procession in gorgeous
vestments and monkish robes carrying banners,
accompanied by boys carrying slow swinging censers.
While she stared amazed, a cloud of incense rose,
obliterating the spectacle, and when it had cleared, the
vision had vanished and only the plain stone pillars
met her eyes. She glanced round anxiously hoping
no one had noticed that she had been asleep, while
she realized that she had gone back five centuries in
her dream, and seen the church as it was then.

' A very dull sermon,' Aunt Marion remarked
drily, as they went out. ' I can't blame you for
taking a nap.'

' I had such a strange dream,' Pauline told her,
' and it seemed so real,' and still half in that older
world which she had glimpsed, she started to describe it, then remembering whom she was with, she

broke off with an apology. Anthony was staring at her in surprise.

'What a vivid imagination you have,' he exclaimed. 'You made me see what you saw. What a picture it would make—"Thomas Spring, Master builder" and that,' he indicated the building in front of him, 'would be the final shot—his glorious achievement.'

'He didn't actually build it himself and it wasn't completed during his lifetime,' Aunt Marion gently corrected him, while Pauline stared at him with a sense of outrage. She had seen few films, and those had not been very good ones; she found them artificial. Her father, caring only for sport, was contemptuous of all art forms, and their creators he designated the scum of the earth, some of his attitude had rubbed off on his daughter. She said in a quivering voice,

'What a dreadful idea! Do you want to see something that was, and still is, sacred, commercialized? Can't you let poor Thomas rest in his grave?'

Anthony was again astonished. 'You're a bit behind the times, aren't you?' he suggested. 'I didn't intend any irreverence. Films, especially on T.V., are one way of showing our heritage to the masses. Tavenham doesn't only belong to you, Miss Herald.'

She turned away, biting her lip. 'I . . . I didn't mean that,' she murmured, 'but it's bad enough having the place overrun with tourists. Does the church have to be cheapened too?'

He was walking close beside her, and determined to widen the distance between them, she quickened her steps, not noticing in her confusion where she was treading, and she stumbled over a pile of flints which workmen doing a minor repair had left by the side of the path. Instantly his arm was round her, steadying her, drawing her back on to the path. There was magnetism in his touch and in every nerve she became aware of the close contact, and when he withdrew his hold, only to draw her arm through his, she was voiceless to protest.

'Until you've quite woken up, you'd better hang on to me,' he said.

Some acquaintances passed them, and bowed, throwing them curious glances. She could guess their thoughts. Pauline Herald with a man in tow, making the most of her chances with the new owner of Three Chimneys! She longed to call to them that she hated him, that he was a usurper and her taskmaster, but why, oh, why did his touch create such havoc with her senses? She made an ineffectual movement to withdraw her arm.

'Really, I'm quite all right. I don't know why I was so stupid.'

He took no notice of her remark, only pressed her arm closer to his side. She suspected that he was enjoying her embarrassment and she wanted to slap his face.

He released her while he unlocked the car, and she shot into the back seat, leaving her aunt to get in sedately in front.

'How red your face is,' Lynette remarked wonderingly as she joined her.

Pauline could have cheerfully slapped her too. She reflected thankfully that her engagements would keep her out of Anthony's way for the rest of the day and he had not arranged to lunch with them.

When he left in the early evening she was taking youthful Dianas over the jumps in the paddock.

and she had not again encountered him. Yet her glance kept straying to the road through the village, and when she saw the distinctive shape of the black Jaguar speeding up the hill, her grey eyes were wistful.

CHAPTER IV

George had absented himself all the weekend, but on the Monday night he came round and found Pauline absorbed in her account books. He came tentatively into the study, but she barely greeted him.

'I can't talk to you now,' she said. 'I've got to make these figures balance.'

The reading lamp on the desk illuminated her bent bright head, and the open book in front of her.

'But it's getting late, Lina,' he protested. 'You mustn't let Ant work you too hard.'

She leaned back in her chair, pushing her hair out of her eyes with a sigh. 'I've got to learn to be disciplined and efficient.'

'Lina,' he began earnestly, 'you can't be enjoying all this,' he indicated the books and scribbled scraps of working paper. 'If only you'd . . .'

She held up a warning hand. 'Please, George, don't ! '

It was his turn to sigh. ' I thought perhaps you'd like to come out for a spin, it's a lovely night with a harvest moon.' He had by no means accepted her refusal as final and hoped persistence might win in the end.

' It's too late, I have to be up early,' she returned, ' thanks all the same.'

He sat down in one of the armchairs and made a great to-do of lighting his pipe, while he watched her covertly. She was looking thinner and paler, he thought. Anthony expected too much from her, forgetting all she had been through. She too was busy with her thoughts; she knew George had not given up hope, and he represented a way out if her position became impossible. For the hundredth time she went over in her mind the episode at Tavenham. The memory brought a feeling of shame, and something else, she was not sure what. Outside an owl was calling, and its mate began to answer, the scent of stock and lavender drifted in from the window. She felt restless and half inclined to accept George's invitation after all, but it was not fair to encourage him if she meant to continue to refuse him. She closed her book with a bang, and swivelled round in her chair to face him. He was sitting where Anthony had sat, and she marvelled that two males of the same species could look so different.

' How do you get on with Ant ? ' he asked.

She was glad the desk lamp was behind her, for she knew she was blushing.

' All right, but I don't like him,' she said, and believed she spoke truth.

George was relieved, but unwisely continued to pursue the subject.

' Any particular reason ? '

She narrowed her eyes. ' Too dictatorial,' she said carelessly, then with a burst of candour, ' I feel as if I were back at school with one of those beastly sarcastic teachers I always loathed.'

George laughed. ' That's a new role for Ant. Always thought he was a bit of a charmer myself. Most women seem to think so.'

Pauline's interest quickened. ' He . . . he's got lots of girl-friends ? ' she asked, and hoped her tone sounded casual.

' Dozens.'

' Any particular one ? ' she persisted.

' Well, I don't know who's the current woman, unless it's still Viola, and she was an eyeful, I can tell you.'

' You've met her ? '

' Saw her once in London, it was at . . .' he stopped, remembering that he had made a promise to Anthony which he was nearly betraying.

' It was . . . where ? ' she prompted.

' Really I don't remember exactly. Why are you so interested ? '

' I'm not,' she lied. ' Mr Marsh's lady-friends are no concern of mine.'

' He likes 'em smart and sophisticated,' George told her. Involuntarily she glanced down at her worn jodhpurs, her usual costume.

' No wonder he thinks I'm just a schoolgirl,' she said a little sadly.

' You must seem so to him, since he's quite a few years older than you are. Besides, I told him . . .' George stopped and reddened.

Pauline looked at him suspiciously. ' You didn't by any chance say I was your girl ? '

He became busy with his pipe, which had gone out.

' Did you, George ? '

' Well . . . er . . .'

' You'd no right to do that ! ' she said indignantly.

' I thought it as well,' he said defensively, ' in case Ant gets ideas.'

' But you've just said he thinks I'm a schoolgirl,' she reminded him, aware that she had blushed again, ' and you say he likes sophisticated girls.'

' Yes—well, propinquity does funny things some-times,' he said, ' and if Viola's being difficult—she often is—he may be looking round for sympathy. All this,' he made a wide gesture, embracing the room, the rising moon visible through the uncur-tained window, the vine leaves in the verandah etched black against its silver, 'makes a charming setting for your pretty face, my dear, and he might be tempted to play nymphs and shepherds, so remember that he *is* only playing, and don't lose your heart to him. Anyway, I mean to keep an eye on him. I'd hate you to be hurt, Lina.'

'Dear George,' she said with assumed lightness, 'you're talking absolute nonsense. I can't see myself falling for Anthony Marsh. He . . . he's a bit of a cissy, you're much more my type. However, thanks for the warning.'

As she saw the gratification on his face, her heart smote her, for what she had said was not quite true. She would never fall for George and she had an uneasy feeling that she might succumb to Anthony, which was absurd, she told herself fiercely, because she hated him, forgetting that hate was the reverse side of love, and whatever she felt, she could never be indifferent to him.

When Anthony came again he brought a friend with him, and she did not see him at all. Aunt Marion waited on them, but they were out most of both days in the Jaguar. Pauline, when she was in the house, found herself listening for the sound of his voice, and watching for a glimpse of his tall figure, and was furious with herself for feeling disappointed when he did not appear.

A fortnight later he came alone and asked if he might have lunch with the family. This time Pauline needed no bidding to put on her green dress. He was polite and friendly during the meal, but his thoughts seemed to be elsewhere. Once, when Lynette had to repeat a question, he apologized.

'Forgive me, my thoughts are far away.'

'In London?' she asked.

'No. With Thomas Spring of Tavenham. My friend who came for a weekend was very taken with the village. Quite a showplace, isn't it?'

So that was where they had spent their time!

'It seems I started something,' Aunt Marion remarked.

'Yes, Miss Thorne, you did,' he told her gravely. 'I can't say yet what, but believe me, it could be quite momentous.'

Though the others were plainly curious, Pauline changed the subject; she did not want to provoke another clash with her employer and knew Tavenham was a thorny subject. But in spite of her resolutions, for she had decided to keep a tight hold on herself, and treat him with cool detachment, a further explosion occurred later in the afternoon. Pegasus had not had sufficient exercise, moreover, a horse is very susceptible to his rider's feelings, and Anthony's proximity had made Pauline nervous and tense. So far all had gone well. He had praised her book-keeping, a rush of pupils had put a sizeable sum in the bank, work on the house was proceeding apace and the garden, with cut lawns and weeded beds, looked trim and tidy, with the disinterred dahlias making splashes of colour everywhere. Having a free hour, she meant to take Pegasus for a gallop to relieve his feelings and her own tension. The big horse was full of oats and high spirits, and chose to take exception to a workman's barrow left near the side gate. Nothing, eyes and ears declared, would induce him to pass that dangerous object which, as he correctly surmised, had no right to be there. In the battle that followed, he gave a fine display of what an obstinate animal can do; rearing, to receive a blow from Pauline's crop on his head, lashing out with his heels, dancing and curveting, rolling his eyes, arching his black crest against the pull of the bit. To an onlooker the scene was terrifying, and onlookers there were. Anthony had come down from the rose garden with Lynette in time to witness this exhibition of Pegasus' temper. He went quite white as he watched the slight, boyish figure clinging to the black brute's back, and Lynette clutched his arm in her fear.

' I wish she wouldn't ride him,' she said nervously. ' He's too big and strong for her. One day he'll throw her.'

' She won't ride him again,' Anthony said grimly.

Pegasus decided that he had made sufficient protest and dashed out of the open gate. They could hear his hooves thundering up the lane at a gallop. Lynette shuddered. ' What'll happen if she meets a car ? '

' Oh, I expect she'll be all right,' Anthony reassured her with a confidence he did not feel. It had been bad enough meeting Pegasus in that lane when he was being led at a walk !

Pauline returned an hour later with a subdued and sweating horse. She stabled him, rubbed him down, and, when he had cooled off, fed him.

' That's better, isn't it old boy ? ' she said. The horse, his daemon exorcized, muzzled her with his soft nose, blowing into her sweater.

She went into the house, tired but soothed. Anthony called to her from the office doorway as she started to go upstairs.

' I'm glad to see you're still in one piece.'

She looked at him in surprise. ' Why shouldn't I be ? '

' I've never in all my life seen such an exhibition. Come in, I want to speak to you.'

Slightly apprehensive, she followed him into the little room, wondering what had gone wrong. The sunlight through the vine leaves on the verandah filled it with greenish light; she supposed that was what was making him look so pale.

'Never again, Miss Herald, are you to ride that horse.' If he had not been so shaken by what he had seen, he might not have spoken so abruptly.

She stared at him wide-eyed, unable to believe her ears.

'Not ride Pegasus?'

'Yes, I believe that's the creature's name. He's no fit mount for a woman. Leave him to Michael.'

The warm colour flooded her face. 'Mr Marsh, you're being absurd. Pegasus was a little fresh this afternoon, but he's not vicious, and I can manage him. You don't know anything about horses. I suppose you thought he was dangerous?'

'Thought? He darned well is! I'm serious, Miss Herald, you're not to ride him.'

Her mouth grew sulky. 'That's ridiculous—Mike isn't keen on riding him.'

'Can't say I blame Mike. In that case he'll have to be sold.'

'Oh no, please!'

'Very well, then. You'll have to persuade Mike to exercise him, but if I find you've disobeyed me, he goes.'

Her temper boiled over. 'Oh, you're being hateful! You're only doing this because you like to bully me. Pegasus would never throw me—I can ride, and I've always ridden him. You think because you're master here you can tyrannize over me, but you can't. I'll go, I won't stop!'

'If you go, so does Pegasus.'

'Oh!' She had always dreaded the horse being

sold. Where she had been flushed, she now turned white, and her eyes were nearly black.

' You know you've got me there,' she said bitterly, ' but you're being mean and unfair.'

He caught hold of her shoulders and shook her.

' Don't you see I want to stop you breaking your pretty neck, you little idiot ! '

She went rigid under his hands. ' It's my own neck,' she flung at him.

' No, it isn't. You're in my employ and if I let you run unnecessary risks I might find myself liable for heavy damages.'

' Oh, I see ! ' And she had for a moment thought he was genuinely concerned for her safety ! Her eyes flashed. ' My mistake, I'm not used to dealing with people who think only in terms of L.S.D.'

' You're impossible ! ' He pulled her towards him, and then suddenly his arms were round her and his lips on hers. Fire seemed to run through her veins, and she went limp in his arms, clinging to him for support. Then, very gently, he put her from him, letting her slip down into one of the old worn chairs. She sat there quivering, trying to subdue her wildly beating heart, while he stared down at her, conscience-stricken.

' I'm sorry,' he said at length, ' I shouldn't have done that, but you're such a little spitfire. ' Unwillingly he smiled. ' You'd provoke an angel,' he added softly, ' for all you're still such a child.'

She drew her hand across her brows, realizing that he had not meant anything by that sudden caress. It had not affected him as it had done her, because he was used to kissing pretty girls when the fancy took him, but she had never been kissed before. As her heartbeats subsided, she smiled at him a little ruefully.

71

'You didn't kiss me as if I were a child.'

He laughed. 'I've apologized, but I don't in the least regret it.'

'Even though I'm George's girl?'

She did not quite know why she said it; perhaps some instinct of self-preservation prompted her, or a desire to provoke him further. His face darkened, but he said conventionally:

'George is a very lucky man.'

Pauline sighed; she had hoped for a more positive reaction, but of course it was nothing to him whose girl she was.

'George doesn't mind me riding Pegasus.'

'Have you ever asked his opinion?'

She had the grace to blush, remembering what George had said when she had asked him to buy the horse. It was the only request of hers that he had ever refused. Anthony's face had grown stern again.

'I meant what I said, Pauline. You may twist George round your little finger, but you won't twist me.' The use of her name gave her unexpected pleasure. Her mouth twitched into an unwilling smile.

'That's why I dislike you so much,' she said.

He came nearer, his eyes holding hers. 'You didn't react as if you disliked me.'

'Oh!' Disconcerted, she jumped to her feet. 'Anyway it doesn't matter, does it? May I go now?'

'If you wish.'

'Thank you.'

She sped to the door, but as she opened it, she looked back at him. He was standing watching her with an unfathomable expression in his hazel eyes, and again her heart began to beat fast. She went out quickly, closing the door behind her.

Pauline and Michael's weekly wage was little more than pocket money after they had paid their aunt for their keep, but Michael managed to save enough out of his to acquire a battered motor-cycle, which, with George's help, he had made roadworthy. Since he wanted to be away in the evenings on his own amusements, he resented having to exercise Pegasus in addition to his other duties.

'Can't you put him out to grass?' he suggested.

Pauline pointed out that Anthony had made no arrangement for renting the field her father had used, and in any case the horse could not be left out all winter.

'He's a useless brute,' Michael grumbled. 'Mr Marsh had the right idea about him.'

'Mike, how can you?' Pauline was shocked.

'Well, then ride him yourself, the boss won't know.'

Though deploring Michael's lack of conscience, she was strongly tempted to disobey Anthony's orders, but to her irritation he made a point of ringing up every evening; his first question always related to Pegasus, and she knew she was incapable of lying to him. She resented this spying, as she termed it, and sought to express her contempt in the shortness of her replies.

'Still spitting fire and brimstone?' he asked on the third occasion, and there was laughter in his voice. To her annoyance Pauline found herself giggling in response. She tried being absent when he called, but he only rang again later and her aunt took her to task, telling her it was her duty to be on hand when her employer wished for a report on her day's work, which made her still more angry, but

73

by the end of the week she discovered she was looking forward to hearing that clear, well modulated voice over the wire, and on the Friday she tried to plead with him.

'Haven't you punished me long enough?' she asked. 'Poor Pegasus misses our gallops and Mike's been very tiresome about taking him out. Really he looks much worse than he is, as you'd know if you were a horseman.' · She could not resist that dig at him.

'I'm not punishing you,' Anthony said drily, 'and though I'm not a horseman, I know horsewomen should be able to control their mounts.'

Pauline gave a gasp of indignation. 'If you mean me, I did . . .'

He cut in with, 'Galloping on the road is not done, and it's bad for his hooves.' She wondered where he had gleaned that information. 'However,' he went on, 'the problem of Pegasus is about to be solved. I'm bringing a man down with me to-morrow.'

Her indignation was drowned in apprehension. 'A . . . a man? Mr Marsh, you're not going to sell him?'

He laughed at the alarm in her voice. 'Not so long as you behave yourself. This chap, Joshua Halliday, is quite a find—ex-jockey, ex-trainer, ex-everything equestrian. I think you need help in the stables and I want his opinion of Pegasus.'

With her new-found regard for expense, she said anxiously, 'Can the business afford extra help?'

'Don't worry about that, he'll be my liability. Incidentally, I'm having a week's holiday, next week, so will you please not make any bookings? I intend to employ you in another capacity.'

'Oh, what?' she asked doubtfully, but he had

rung off.

Pauline too had saved up her money. She meant to buy a new pair of jodhpurs, but after a shopping expedition into Bury, she returned with a new suit. Exactly what had urged her to buy it she could not say, except that the weather was becoming too chilly for her green crimplene, and she had nothing else that was presentable to wear during Anthony's visits.

He duly arrived on the Saturday morning accompanied by Joshua Halliday and Josh Junior, who was called Jo to distinguish him from his father. Josh was small and wiry with the typical horseman's face, long, lean and leathery. Jo, aged about nine, was a miniature replica of his sire. What had happened to Mrs Halliday, nobody seemed to know. Anthony had arranged for them to lodge at the farm across the road from Three Chimneys whence Jo could go to school on the bus with the farmer's flaxen-haired brood. At Anthony's request Michael and Pauline showed Josh round the stables and the harness room. He made no comment whatever, merely sucked a straw, while his small grey eyes darted here and there, missing nothing. Finally they came to Pegasus, and Anthony, who had joined them, asked Pauline to lead him out into the yard. The little man's face lighted up enthusiastically.

'Some horse!' he ejaculated.

He came up to Pegasus, looking little more than a dwarf beside the animal's bulk, and took the head-stall from Pauline's unwilling hand. He ran a claw-like hand over the horse's neck and shoulder, then very methodically, he examined him from head to tail, feeling his hocks, raising each of his feet in turn, speaking all the while in a crooning voice, while Pegasus quivered, but made no objection.

An affinity seemed to have been born between them. Finally Josh straightened himself, and looked at Anthony.

'You've got summat here, mister. Look at them quarters—reckon he can jump sky-high. If I can have the training of him I'll make a champion of him, I promise you.'

'He'll be entirely in your hands,' Anthony told him, while Pauline felt a pang, remembering her own hopes for Pegasus. Anthony glanced at her with understanding.

'Josh knows all the ropes,' he told her. 'He's going to teach Pegasus to be a show jumper. It's a pity to waste his talents, don't you think?'

She nodded, and turned away, biting her lower lip to still its quivering; it had always been a pipe dream that she herself could show Pegasus at Wembley, but Josh had the know-how, and she had not. It was Josh who led Pegasus back into his box, and she felt like a mother who has seen her son depart for his first term at boarding school.

Josh departed with his offspring to settle in at the farm, and Anthony took Pauline into the office, the scene of all their clashes, to explain to her the new set-up. Josh with Michael's help was to do all the stable work, while she was to confine herself to organization and instruction.

'I shan't earn my keep,' she protested.

'Yes, you will, you will deputise for me in my absence, but this coming week, I want you to have a holiday. Josh can take over your pupils, and I want you and your aunt to show me your country.'

'I don't want a holiday . . .' she was beginning, when he cut her short.

'That's a pity, because that's my order.' He looked at her reproachfully. 'Must you always force me to act the tyrant ? '

' You're not acting,' she informed him. ' It comes natural.'

He laughed, but his laughter had an edge to it. ' Did your father ever smack you ? ' he asked.

She looked surprised. ' Not that I can remember. Why ? '

' Because a good smacking would do you a world of good,' he said grimly. ' Okay, that's all for now. Be ready to accompany me and your aunt on Monday morning.'

He held the door open for her with exaggerated courtesy and she walked out with dignity and heightened colour, reflecting, not for the first time, that if there were any chastisement to be administered, how much she would enjoy slapping that smooth handsome face.

The next day, although it was Sunday, was a busy one, as Josh had to be shown where everything was, and Anthony, with Aunt Marion's help, was arranging the new furniture that had come down from London for his sitting room. Young Jo trotted round at his father's heels, and was highly delighted when his father put him up on one of the ponies.

' He's a rare 'un for horses,' Josh chuckled proudly. ' Reckon he were born in the saddle.'

The child was shy and tongue-tied, except with Lynette. To her he chattered volubly, but Pauline never discovered what about. Lynette was evasive; she had for the first time in her life found a friend of her own, and did not want to share him, but that was a development of the days to come. Meanwhile, on Monday morning Pauline woke to recollect with mingled pleasure and distress—she still felt vaguely demoted—that she need not get up early and rush out to the stables in her ancient jodhpurs. Instead

77

she could dress herself leisurely in her new suit and frilly blouse, the short skirt of the former showing a length of slender shapely leg, normally concealed, and go down to an unhurried breakfast. They were enjoying a spell of bright, sunny weather, which often came in early autumn, and Anthony meant to make the most of it. He had asked Lynette to join their expedition, but she preferred to stop at home, ostensibly to look after Mike. Aunt Marion found an opportunity to tell him that, although she would not admit it, she knew Lynette was nervous in cars since her father's accident, so that he did not press his invitation.

Pauline thought that she too should have developed a phobia, but as she entered the back seat of the Jaguar, her spirits began to rise. It was months since she had been off the premises, except for a rare shopping excursion and the prospect of revisiting many well-loved haunts was not uninviting.

Their road lay through Melford, equidistant with Tavenham, but in the opposite direction, where the beautiful church stands above the sloping village green and the long tree-bordered street is lined with houses of every age—timbered like the ancient Bull Inn, complete with ghost, combining antiquity with expensive comfort, the Tudor chimneys rising above the red brick of Melford Hall, and bow-windowed shops alongside Georgian mansions. Suffolk is a county of picturesque villages and small market towns, of sleepy rivers widening to broad estuaries, of forests and heathlands, wide skies and desolate marshes, presenting a variety of landscapes to the explorer. Passing through Sudbury, centre of a silk industry originally introduced to support the weavers left unemployed by the decline of the wool trade, with its tall church tower overlooking the market square; they ran along the Suffolk side of the Stour, which divides two counties, lying in the shallow valley which is the Constable country. At Flatford Mill they left the car in the field provided for parking and walked past the Mill to admire Willie Lot's cottage, limewashed and red-roofed, like so many Suffolk cottages, where they tried to reconstruct ' The Hay-Wain ' but found the trees and vegetation much changed since the artist's day, if indeed his picture had been a faithful reproduction. Retracing their steps, they crossed the old wooden bridge over the river, here green as pea soup, and walked under willow trees, dripping pale golden leaves into the water. Aunt Marion had packed a picnic lunch, which they ate sitting on a low wall facing the Mill across the millpond, while a flotilla of ducks descended upon them to claim their toll. The warm October sun poured down upon them, and as it was late in the year there were few tourists to disturb their peace.

Pauline surreptitiously watched Anthony as he threw bread to the ducks, and expressed delight at the antics of a pair of moorhens bobbing about under the opposite bank. Wearing an open-necked pullover, he looked young and boyish, and it was difficult to reconcile his appearance with the stern taskmaster of their first acquaintanceship. Turning from the water fowl as if he felt her gaze upon him, he met her eyes; she made a charming picture sitting upon the low wall, her green jumper—she had discarded her jacket—and red-brown hair toning with the greens and golds of the foliage and water behind her. She turned her head away and moved uneasily under his close regard.

' What's the matter ?   Have I laddered my stocking or got a smut on my nose ? ' she asked defiantly.

' Neither. I was thinking how charming you look and how, if I were John Constable, I'd whip out my palette and paints and make a picture of you.'

She stood up, shaking the crumbs from her skirt. ' Study of a country mouse? ' she suggested.

' Most inappropriate. Mice, according to Robbie Burns, were "wee timorous beasties".' He glanced at her long, slim legs. ' Dryad would be better.'

' What's a dryad ? '

Aunt Marion looked up from collecting the debris of their meal, a chore it was only too evident other visitors had neglected. ' A wood nymph,' she told her.

' Oh.' Pauline supposed the comparison was a compliment, but it was too flowery to please her. George would have told her that she looked nice without any fancy work.

Mistley was their next objective, since the estuary represented another aspect of the Suffolk scene; they drove through the narrow street of the little town, and drew up under some trees, with a stretch of cut grass between them and the water, which was alive with swans. Some were slithering about in the mud left by the receding tide, looking clumsy and awkward, but further out they were swimming gracefully, looking like a cloud of white foam. Far down the river, Parkeston Quay was just visible, while across the estuary in front of them rose low rolling slopes, decked with trees and hedges in their gorgeous autumn garb, fading into a blue distance, and above it all was the tremendous arc of the sky, where small white clouds crossed the limitless blue.

Next day they decided to go to the coast, and finished up at Aldeburgh, where they explored the quaint old Guildhall, which had defied time and tide, more than once it had been flooded, and survived as a museum. They walked along the sea wall towards the yacht station. It was here that the River Alde, having almost reached the sea, turns southwards, leaving a long tongue of shingle beach between it and its ultimate destination. This was a place that had been fully exploited by smugglers in olden times, but now housed a nature reserve and an R.A.F. station. The river, which was tidal at this point, carried a fleet of small boats with blue and white sails, looking like a flight of butterflies skimming over its surface, though many had been beached awaiting the return of their owners next summer. A stiffish breeze was blowing off the sea, which made Pauline shiver in her thin suit, though it brought the bright colour to her cheeks, and tangled her bright hair, so that she was not sorry when they returned to the shelter of the street. Anthony stood them an excellent lunch in a pseudo-Elizabethan restaurant, playing the attentive host with courtesy and charm. They might have been V.I.P.s instead of his employees. She wondered why he was doing it—surely he could have found more congenial company among his own friends with which to spend his holiday ? She could not believe that Aunt Marion's, to her, rather boring information about the places they visited could be really interesting to him, although he listened patiently, and any way he could have found it all in the guide books. Often she found his eyes upon her with a questioning look, as if he were wondering what sort of a creature lived behind her somewhat prickly exterior, but she was not vain enough to think that she attracted him. She was glad that her aunt's age and dignity obtained for her the front seat in the car. At the back, she felt less constrained by Anthony's proxi-

mity, which continued to be disturbing. In spite
of all her efforts to keep it alive; her antagonism was
fading. She did not want to be friends with the
usurper who had taken over Three Chimneys, but
she could not wholly hold aloof from his friendliness
and the magic of those golden days spent in his company. When they were over, she supposed he would
revert into the stern employer she was determined
to dislike, meanwhile, she must concede to this
strange whim of his, and accept the new aspect of
him with good grace. That he might consider she
needed a break after all her tribulations never crossed
her mind, for kindness was not an attribute she
would have connected with Anthony Marsh.

It seemed he was not drawn to castles, saying
there were much finer ones in Wales, he had been
to the Investiture at Caernarvon, (trying to impress
us, was Pauline's inward comment) so neither the
curtain wall at Framlingham nor the Norman keep
at Orford attracted him, but the churches were a
different matter. Suffolk churches were as fine as
any in the country.

They went as far as Southwold, which possessed
one of the most beautiful. The original painted
screen still retained some of its gilding, and the star-
spangled roof of the chancel was painted the colour
of heaven, the hammer beams terminating in gilded
angels. They stopped to look at Blythburgh, where
the little winding river Blyth widens to a tidal
estuary haunted by sea-birds including herons, a
place that long ago had once been a flourishing seaport. Here was another great, gaunt church, and
an ancient inn, memorials to an age long past.
Thence they went over Dunwich heath, where gorse
still bloomed among the dead heath and heather,
and the bracken was brown and golden. The road

to the sea led through another forest, into Dunwich, the forlorn remains of the one-time principal seaport of East Anglia. They left the car and stood on the crumbling cliffs, looking out over the grey waters that had devoured a whole city, and where, it was fabled, the bells of the drowned churches could be heard ringing in stormy weather.

'Though that is just a tale,' Aunt Marion said. 'Divers have been down and there's nothing there except sand.'

'Roman coins have been washed up on the beach,' Pauline commented, 'and . . . other things.' She shivered.

'What other things?' Anthony was interested.

'Where we're standing is the churchyard,' Aunt Marion told him. 'The church went over bit by bit, the last piece not so long ago. Now there are only the graves left. Every year a bit more is washed away, including the bones, which you can pick up on the beach.'

'Let's go.' Pauline shivered again; the sun had gone behind a cloud and the wind blew cold; behind her a stone wall separated them from a large enclosure, in the centre of which part of a ruined building stood, all that was left of Grey Friars Priory, and it was used to house pigs! 'This place is too desolate,' she said, 'and too old. I think there must be ghosts at night.'

'That vivid imagination of yours?' Anthony asked. He was looking at her curiously. This girl was a mass of contradictions, one moment a termagant, the next, a visionary.

'Perhaps,' she smiled wanly, 'and the sea isn't the only threat. If that place blew up there'd be greater havoc than even the sea has wrought.' She pointed southwards to where a dim grey shape showed through the gathering mist.

' That ? What's that ? '

' Sizewell Atomic Power Station,' Aunt Marion said briskly. ' Lina, you're getting morbid.'

' She's cold,' Anthony suggested. ' Come on, Pauline, race you down the hill.'

He easily outdistanced her, and was waiting as she reached the end of the steep, grassy slope.

' I can't stop ! '

She ran straight into his arms, and for an instant he held her close; she thought his lips touched her hair.

' The next thing is to find a hot cup of tea,' he said, turning towards the car, but his voice was not quite steady, or did she imagine it ? She herself was in the hopeless state of confusion that any contact with Anthony always produced in her and she was glad to hide herself in the back of the car, while they waited for Aunt Marion to complete her more sedate descent.

That night she decided that she wanted no more of his company. If, as George had suggested, he wanted to play nymphs and shepherds, she was not going to partner him. In future he could go alone with her aunt, who knew much more about the county than she did, but when she suggested to him that she should resume her neglected duties, she met with a stern refusal.

' Do you never give up ? ' he asked her. ' I said a week's holiday and I meant it. Already you look much better for the break, so don't let me have any more nonsense about staying at home.'

He was right there. She had lost the drawn look that used to come into her face when she was over-tired, her eyes were brighter and her skin glowed. That there was another reason for her bloom beyond

84

the rest and fresh air, she would not admit even to herself, although she did realize that she was unexpectedly glad that he had refused to let her withdraw from their expeditions.

On the last day they went to Christchurch Park, where the fine Elizabethan mansion has been turned into a museum. There they found the portrait of Margaret Catchpole, whose story had always intrigued Pauline, and she told it to Anthony. How Margaret had risked her life and been imprisoned because of her love for the smuggler Will Laud. How, during their final effort to escape, with the boat that was to take them to safety almost within reach, Will had been shot by a Preventive Man, and had died on the beach at her feet. Margaret herself had been arrested and again tried, the sentence of death being commuted to deportation to Australia. Her romancers had contrived a happy marriage for her in that country, but in actual fact she remained unwed, faithful to the memory of her wild lover. The picture showed a dark, handsome woman, with fine eyes.

'Rather wasted on a smuggler,' Anthony remarked, 'but women always seem to have a soft spot for bad lots.'

'At least Will was a man, not like the hippies and layabouts we have nowadays.'

'They had their wastrels in those days, too,' he looked at her oddly. 'You admire men of action, don't you? You think more of Josh Halliday than myself?'

She had to laugh as she contrasted Josh's wizened form with the tall well-dressed figure beside her.

'Don't let's be personal,' she evaded.

'Well, then let's say Will Laud appeals to you more than John Constable?'

'I don't know a thing about artistic people,' she told him. 'They all seem rather half men to me.'

'Indeed?'

'I couldn't be interested in anyone who couldn't sit a horse,' she said wickedly.

'So I imagined,' he said curtly. They left the house in silence, outside the sun was shining brightly on the smooth lawns and fine trees.

'Shall we look at the arboretum?' Aunt Marion suggested.

'I think we'd better be getting home,' Anthony returned shortly.

Pauline knew she had needled him. She had done it deliberately. It might well be that he had artistic aspirations himself, for he had talked about making a film of Tavenham, but surely her opinions could not really matter to him?

On Sunday morning he took them again to Tavenham, and after the service, he lingered to inspect the monuments and the beautiful carving of the Spring chantry. The place seemed to fascinate him, but he made no comment, and she was careful not to stumble when they went out to the car.

'All good things have to come to an end,' he said regretfully, as he opened the door for her. 'Your holiday has done you good, my dear.'

She flushed at the familiarity of the last two words, and her aunt said quickly, 'Yes, but now it's time we all got back to work.' Her shrewd eyes had been watching the two young people, and she was not happy at what she had noticed during the week. She thought that it was high time Anthony went back to Town.

He sighed. 'I shan't be able to get away for several weekends, I'm afraid.'

Excellent, Aunt Marion thought, while Pauline

experienced a sinking heart.

When they dróve into the drive at Three Chimneys they found a strange car parked outside the front door. Anthony gave it one look and accelerated into the yard, nearly colliding with the dividing wall. Glancing at his face, Pauline saw thunder about his brows. Evidently he had recognized the car and the visitor was unwelcome.

He went striding away round to the front of the house, and her curiosity aroused, she followed. All the windows were open to the October sun, and as she stepped into the verandah, she could hear the murmur of voices in Anthony's room. Michael was with the visitor, and she heard him say apologetically :

' I thought I'd better bring her in here and I couldn't very well leave her alone.'

Anthony's voice floated out to her, quick and sharp.

' What on earth brings you here, Viola ? '

Then a woman's, low and husky, ' To see your hideout, Tony darling.'

Viola ? George's words came back to her. ' I don't know who's the current woman, unless it's still Viola.'

Apparently it was still Viola, and she had called Anthony ' darling '. Pauline hurriedly left the verandah. She had heard enough; she felt a little sick.

CHAPTER V

Having no wish to encounter Anthony's girl-friend, Pauline took refuge in the paddock, accompanied by Duchess, who was always on the look-out for a walk. While the dog worked along the hedgerows, hoping to dislodge a stray rabbit, the girl watched the distant road through the village, and her vigilance was rewarded by the sight of the Jaguar speeding up the hill. Anthony had gone and she told herself that she hoped he would not be returning, and that she was glad that Viola had arrived to claim her man, so that his attention would be directed away from herself and her doings, and she could get on with her work without interruption. But she could not quite suppress the niggling little ache in her heart, which was quite uncalled for. She supposed it was a lingering regret for the days of pleasant holiday which had abruptly terminated.

She was calm and composed when she came in to lunch to learn that Anthony had taken his visitor into Melford for a meal, much to the relief of Aunt Marion, who did not feel that her commissariat would be up to Miss Sylvester's probably exacting standards.

'Sylvester?' Pauline asked. 'Is that her name? Viola Sylvester—sounds like an actress.'

'She is an actress,' Michael confirmed, 'and she's simply gorgeous. I suppose she's engaged to Mr Marsh. That guy's got everything.'

'You don't know that,' Aunt Marion began, glancing doubtfully at Pauline's carefully controlled face. 'He didn't seem very pleased to see her.'

'Perhaps he thought she wouldn't appreciate

Three Chimneys,' Pauline suggested. Viola did not sound the sort of girl who would fancy a place in the country. 'But she is his girl, George said so.'

After lunch the ubiquitous Miss Frasers appeared, and Pauline would gladly have gone out with them in Michael's stead, if she had not known that they would not appreciate the exchange. Owing to Anthony's interdict, she had no bookings of her own, and she wandered restlessly about the house and garden seeing every now and again the blue car parked in front of the house, an unpleasant reminder that Viola would return. Aunt Marion, glad of a chance to relax, had settled down with a book. Lynette had gone off somewhere with Jo, and she knew Josh would not welcome her in the stables, she felt unwanted and superfluous.

She was disconsolately picking up the fallen leaves from under the vine when the Jaguar came in at the gate and pulled up behind the blue car. An irresistible desire to see Anthony's girl kept her where she was, hoping they would not notice her. Anthony jumped out and came round to open the door, holding out his hand to help his companion to alight, and Pauline's heart contracted strangely at the sight of him, elegant and debonair, paying deference to another woman. A slim figure stepped out on to the gravel, bareheaded but wearing sun-glasses, which was an affectation since the sunlight was not strong. Her hair was ash-blonde and she wore pale blue slacks and a tight white sweater, both garments fully revealing her graceful curves. Everything about her was expensive, from her chic hair-style to the blue and white sandals on her small, arched feet. Pauline became acutely conscious that her suit was a cheap ready-made, her hair was ruffled and she wore no make-up. She turned quickly to beat a retreat, but Anthony had seen her.

' Hi! Miss Herald, come here! '

So she was ' Miss Herald ' again; she had been
' Pauline ' all the week! Reluctantly she descended
the two shallow steps leading out of the verandah
and went towards the newcomer. Viola took off her
sun-glasses and stared at Pauline appraisingly, while
Pauline returned her gaze with equal curiosity.
Viola had round blue eyes, but the thick lashes surrounding them were artificial, so too was her carefully put on complexion; she was in fact a perfect
work of art. Her age was nearer to Anthony's
than Pauline's, but every effort had been expended
to give an illusion of early youth, and she was seeing
youth that was not an illusion, needing no artifice
to enhance it. She ran an experienced eye over
the slender, boyish figure, noting the wide, grey eyes,
the soft mouth and delicate bloom in the younger
girl's cheeks, and felt, what to her was a calamity,
middle-aged.

Anthony introduced them, somewhat unwillingly,
Pauline thought, and Viola said:

' So you're the little Diana who has kept Tony so
long in Arcady? ' She had a husky voice with
something of a drawl, the smile that accompanied
her words was completely insincere. ' I never knew
you cared about horses, Tony.'

' I don't,' he returned, and his voice was very dry,
' except for the occasional flutter. Miss Herald runs
my riding school. Since it was in operation when I
took over, I decided to continue with it.'

' So you've already told me,' the drawl was more
pronounced, ' but I expected Miss Herald to be quite
different. The horsey women I've met before have
always resembled their mounts, and surely you're
very young, my dear, to hold such a responsible

position ? It isn't as if Tony were often here to supervise you.'

'I'm of age,' Pauline said shortly, 'and none of my pupils have thought I was too young to be efficient.'

'I've found Miss Herald perfectly capable,' Anthony added, and for the life of her Pauline could not resist giving Anthony a mischievous glance and saw his eyes were twinkling. Both of them knew the statement was not strictly true. Viola saw the look and her eyes narrowed.

'Yes, well . . .' she waved a languid hand, dismissing Pauline and turning to Anthony. 'Shall we go inside, Tony ? '

At that moment, Michael, having done his duty by the Miss Frasers, came round the corner of the house, and Viola turned back to greet him eagerly.

'Ah, here's my young sportsman ! Hi, Adonis ! ' Michael was looking particularly handsome, for although his breeches were shabby, they were well cut, and his boots were highly polished; he wore an open-necked yellow sweater and his red-brown hair had been carefully combed into regular waves.

'You seem full of classical allusions this afternoon,' Anthony remarked sourly, 'and Adonis, I seem to remember, came to a sticky end.'

'But he was loved by Venus herself.' She went towards Michael, whose face had lighted up at the sight of her. 'I've had a wonderful idea,' she announced. 'Do you think you could teach me to ride ? '

Adonis was enraptured by this Venus. 'I'd be delighted,' he exclaimed fervently.

'But aren't you going back to Town ? ' Anthony asked anxiously.

'I've changed my mind.' She threw him a barbed

glance. 'As you know, I'm resting, and what better place could I find in which to relax? I can put up at that pub where we lunched, and run out here for my lessons.'

Anthony was plainly put out. 'What's the big idea?' he asked abruptly. 'You know you hate country life. You'd be bored stiff.'

'I'm hoping to discover why you find it so attractive,' she said sweetly, 'and I shan't be bored, Michael will see to that. A shame that you've to return tonight.'

Anthony caught hold of her arm and drew her aside, but not quite out of earshot, and Pauline heard him say, 'Viola, for heaven's sake leave that boy alone,' and her reply, 'My dear Tony, you haven't got a monopoly in pastoral diversions.'

They moved further off, while Pauline went to join her brother, anger pulsing through her, evoked by that contemptuous phrase, 'pastoral diversions'. Michael was standing staring after Viola with a bemused expression.

'Do you think she really meant it?' he asked her eagerly. 'She's going to take lessons from me?'

'I haven't a clue,' Pauline snapped, 'but I shouldn't think any of her whims lasted long, and don't forget she's Mr Marsh's girl.'

'He's a bit old for her,' said the besotted youth, who had been completely deceived by Viola's make-up.

'Oh, for crying out loud!' Pauline exclaimed irritably, wondering if she should repeat what she had overheard, but she decided against it. Michael in his present mood would only laugh at her. If Viola intended to make of him her 'pastoral diversion', he would have to learn the hard way. She glanced at the couple under the weeping willow.

Anthony was talking earnestly, but his companion did not seem to be taking him seriously, her light laughter tinkled on the breeze. Nevertheless they were two of a kind, both elegant, sophisticated creatures from another world, between them and herself and Mike, a wide gulf yawned. Unconsciously she sighed as she re-entered the house.

Anthony left soon afterwards, after telling Miss Thorne that he would not be able to come down again for some time. He did not say goodbye to Pauline, who kept out of his way. Michael, who had opened the gate for him, reported that he seemed to be in a vile temper. Viola too took her departure, after arranging that she would come on the following Tuesday for her first lesson, she needed the Monday to buy her riding outfit. Evidently she had won her argument with Anthony, and Michael was in a seventh heaven, but Pauline's heart was heavy with foreboding; she could see no good coming to her brother from associating with the attractive actress. She would have been even more disturbed if she had known what Miss Sylvester was thinking as she drove away.

Viola approved of Anthony's 'place in the country'; it would make a delightful summer residence where they could entertain their friends. The Heralds of course must go, especially the girl, though she had been pleasantly surprised to discover such a simple creature. Anthony rarely mentioned her, which had been a bad sign, and she had feared to find a formidable rival, but Pauline would have no idea of how to compete with an experienced woman. Anthony would soon tire of her naïveté and be agreeable to her dismissal. Meanwhile, the brother was an attractive young savage; he would provide her with considerable amusement, and in return she might help him to escape from his impossible rural environment. It would be good for her figure to learn to ride, and any accomplishment was useful in her profession, and if in the process Tony became jealous, so much the better. He had been falling off in his attentions lately and needed to be brought to heel. She pulled up in the car park of the Melford inn, which in spite of its carefully preserved ancient appearance provided all the comforts which she found essential to her pampered existence, and went in to book her reservation, well pleased with her morning's work.

On Tuesday morning she presented herself at Three Chimneys, in brand new jodhpurs, boots, yellow shirt and hacking jacket, but no hat.

' You ought to have one,' Michael insisted. ' A hard hat protects your head if you have a fall.'

' Dear boy,' she purred, ' I'm sure you won't let me have a fall.'

He mounted her on Bonny, the quietest of the hacks, and they were gone a long time. Josh, who had watched their departure sucking a straw, told the anxious Pauline, ' Not to worrit, them two knows what they're up to, and it in't riding,' which did not reassure her. She had to turn the Miss Frasers over to Josh's guidance, much to their disgust.

The truants returned at long last with remarkably fresh horses and a self-conscious-looking Michael. He cut short Pauline's reproaches with, ' Oh, I knew you'd cope somehow, and I'm sick of those stupid Fraser girls.' He went in to ask his aunt if Viola might stay to lunch. That she had come prepared for the invitation was obvious, for after spending an unconscionable time in the bathroom, she came down in beautifully tailored black trousers, and a

94

black jersey which showed off her carefully put on complexion to perfection. Pauline had not bothered to change, but Michael had put on a clean white shirt, moreover, since Viola had appropriated the bathroom, he had used Anthony's new one and had, from the scent he exuded, helped himself liberally to Anthony's lavender bath salts, a luxury Pauline considered effeminate. Viola during lunch was both witty and entertaining, and Lynette listened enthralled to her stories about studio and stage. She too noticed the absence of a television set.

'Then you won't have seen my last series, "After Nightfall",' she said. 'Really I'm surprised that Tony hasn't installed one, or is there one in his room?'

Aunt Marion told her there was not.

Viola looked put out. 'Most extraordinary. Doesn't he want to keep in touch?'

'What with?' Michael asked.

'Well, there's often an Alhambra production that he directed,' then, seeing their blank faces, 'Didn't you know that Tony was a television director? Mean to say he's never told you what he does?'

'Mr Marsh is very reticent about his affairs,' Pauline said coldly, but she surmised that the reticence had been deliberate, he had not told her, nor let George tell her because he had thought she would despise his work; then she gave herself a mental shake. He had not mentioned his work because they were utterly divorced from his real life, they were a sideline and quite unimportant.

Lynette exclaimed rapturously, 'I knew he couldn't be anything ordinary!'

'There's nothing very wonderful about directing plays and films,' Viola pointed out. She was pleased to discover their ignorance; there could have been

95

no intimate talk between him and the girl. She went on: ' He's trying to interest Ken Latimer—he's one of Alhambra's V.I.P.s—in doing a play about someone called Sprig, or some such name, who built a church. It all sounds pretty drear to me, but Tony gets these odd fancies, thinks they're educational or worth while.' She sounded bored.

Pauline remembered what Anthony had said about showing England's heritage to the masses. So this was what he had had in mind ! Aunt Marion asked:
' Surely that's a laudable aim ? '

Viola yawned. ' The public don't want laudable aims, they want amusement. As for the Sprig thing, if it means going to some outlandish spot for the location shots, I hope to goodness Latimer does turn it down.'

' Would you be in it if it comes off ? ' Michael asked eagerly, anticipating Viola's arrival at Tavenham with the film unit.

' Probably, I'm in most of Alhambra's major productions. I've influence with the management, you see.'

They did not see, nepotism being outside their experience.

' Of course one can't appear too often,' Viola went on, ' except in a series. The public gets tired of the same old faces.'

' I can't imagine any one getting tired of yours,' Michael said gallantly.

' Thank you, dear boy. Unfortunately you aren't everybody.' She was pleased. Viola could lap up any amount of adulation, especially from good-looking young men.

' I was very disappointed when Tony went in for direction,' she went on, ' but I hope very much he'll go back to acting. He could have been an international star today if he'd gone on with it.'

Lynette's eyes grew round. 'You mean Mr Marsh used to be an actor?' she gasped.

'Yes. He comes of a theatrical family. He scored a success in a film called "Passionate Pomegranates", in which I also had a small part.'

Pauline squirmed inwardly. Each revelation Viola made seemed to increase the chasm between Anthony and herself, but this last one did more than open a chasm, it revealed him as being one of those impossible creatures her father had described as 'the scum of the earth'.

'I remember that film,' Aunt Marion said unexpectedly. 'I saw it, but that was a long time ago, he must have been very young.'

'He was, and I was only a schoolgirl,' Viola said quickly, realizing that if Miss Thorne started adding up, she would discover that she was on the wrong side of thirty. Her name then had been Violet Simpson, but since her part had been a very small one, it was unlikely that she would recall that. Pauline had noticed something else.

'You've known Mr Marsh a very long time, then?' she asked.

'Oh, we kept meeting and parting, as one does in our job,' Viola said airily, wishing that in her desire to impress her audience she had not been quite so specific, 'but it's only of later years that we've become really intimate. I still hope to persuade him to come to Hollywood. We were offered a joint engagement, and when he refused it, we had quite a row—in fact we've only just made it up.'

So that was why Anthony had not been pleased to see her. The reconciliation must have occurred during lunch, Pauline decided.

'What sort of film was "Passionate Pomegranates " ? ' Michael asked. ' The only ones I like are Westerns.'

Viola laughed merrily. ' Dear boy, don't be dim, can you imagine Tony as Buffalo Bill ? No, it was a romantic piece and he was hailed as the new great screen lover.'

Pauline pushed aside her plate. ' Excuse me, I must go,' she murmured. Nobody noticed her departure, they were too absorbed in Viola's disclosures, which they found romantic and exciting. But Pauline's principal reaction was revulsion. Bad enough to find out that Anthony was connected with entertainment at all; that he had actually been one of those slick young men who pursue their well tailored way from one amatory adventure to another through the artificial mazes of the celluloid screen repelled her; true, he had given it up, but Viola seemed confident that he would go back to it at her insistence. How could a man who spent his life portraying synthetic emotion ever be sincere ? She did not realize that she was confusing Anthony's screen image with the real person. She had softened towards him during that magical week's holiday, he had seemed genuinely interested in the places they had visited, and—she admitted it—charming if dictorial towards herself, but he had learned how to charm, it was part of his stock in trade, and it had amused him to practise his wiles on herself, evoking in her the response that he expected. Her face burned as she remembered how she had run into his arms at Dunwich, as no doubt he had meant her to do. Viola's words recurred to her; she had been his ' pastoral diversion ' while what genuine feeling, if he had any, was centred on Viola. What a dim little innocent he must believe her to be ! At that moment she heartily wished that she need never see

him again. One consoling fact was that she was
not likely to do so for a long time.

Viola came every day, and often after her lesson
stayed to lunch. She declared that she was grateful
to the Heralds for their hospitality, that she so
enjoyed home cooking and was fed up with hotel
meals. Whether her riding made much progress,
Pauline did not know, but there was no doubt the
family enjoyed her company. She was charmingly
deferential to Miss Thorne, made a pet of Lynette,
and Michael was obviously infatuated. Only
Pauline resented her presence and was worried on
her brother's account.

With the installation of Josh, Anthony had ceased
his daily calls, so that they had no contact with him.
Pauline often felt lonely; even Pegasus had been taken
out of her hands. George called round from time to
time, but she did not think it was fair to encourage
him. He seemed glad that Viola had appeared to
claim her property, having had misgivings about the
wisdom of introducing Anthony to Three Chimneys,
but in his view, Viola was obviously far more suited
to his friend than Pauline, whom no doubt he still
considered a child. Pauline spent a lot of time watching Josh take Pegasus over the jumps he had erected
in the paddock, keeping herself well concealed behind
the hedge, for Josh had told her that she might dis-
tract his charge if he knew of her presence. When
he was not at school, Jo sometimes accompanied her
and confided to her his ambition to be a jockey,
which, since he promised to be small and wiry, it
seeméd he might well attain.

Two weeks passed. Viola's rest seemed to be
becoming extended. She went back to Town at the
weekends, and each time Michael was desolate,
always asking the same question: 'Do you think

she'll come back ? '

To which Pauline would reply: ' She's booked a lesson for next week, hasn't she ? '

' Yes, but when she gets among all those smart, clever people she knows, she may change her mind.'

The smart, clever people who were also Anthony's colleagues ! Pauline used to wonder if Viola regaled them with those cruel, witty remarks of hers at the expense of Three Chimneys and its inmates.

On her return from her second weekend, while she was having lunch, Pauline waited, striving against her longing to hear her mention Anthony, but she did not do so, until Lynette asked timidly:

' Did you see Mr Marsh ? Is he very busy ? '

' Dead to the world,' Viola said shortly, ' absorbed in new plans. You'll not be seeing him for ages, long after I've gone back to Town.' And not then, if I can help it, she added mentally.

But Viola was wrong, for on the following Friday night, when Pauline had unsuspectingly answered the phone, she found Anthony on the line. The unexpected sound of his voice set her heart knocking against her ribs, but she managed to reply flatly to his query about their wellbeing, with a casual:

' Oh, everything's okay, I suppose.'

' It doesn't sound so.' His tone was anxious. ' What's the matter with my little spitfire ? '

She flared up: ' I can't always be going off like a rocket for your amusement ! '

He laughed. ' That sounds more like you ! Is Viola still at Melford ? '

She told him she was. ' And she's been entertaining us with stories about your early career,' she added maliciously, and was pleased to hear him groan.

' What's she been saying ? '

'She told us all about a picture called "Passionate Pomegranates".' She brought out the title on a fine note of scorn.

'That muck?' he exclaimed. 'I've been trying to live it down ever since I was fool enough to let myself be inveigled into doing it, but in those days I couldn't afford to pick and choose.'

'Aunt Marion saw it.'

'Oh, no! Lina,' he used for the first time the name her family called her by, 'I can't give up my profession, it's my trade, but when I get a chance, I do try to do something worth while.'

She wondered why he seemed to be trying to excuse himself to her, as if he could care whether it mattered to her what he did and wherefore.

'I daresay,' and now she really did manage to get the right degree of indifference into her voice, 'but it's no concern of mine.'

There was a silence at the other end of the line, and then he said lightly:

'Don't be too sure about that, I've managed to get quite a bit of support for the idea of the Spring play. If and when the camera team come down to Suffolk, your horses will come in useful, and you yourself for that matter. We'll need extras who can ride.'

'Thank you, but I've no wish to compete with Miss Sylvester.'

'You couldn't,' he said brutally, and that she thought was true in more ways than one. 'I'm paying you a flying visit on Sunday, if I can get away.'

All pretence of indifference vanished. 'Sunday? but you said you wouldn't be coming for ages, and Miss Sylvester said so too.'

'I can't keep away any longer, I must come.'

' To see Miss Sylvester, or on behalf of Mr Thomas Spring ? '

' Neither,' he said firmly. ' To see you.' And hung up.

Pauline stood motionless holding the buzzing microphone to her ear. Could she have heard his last remark aright, or was it his idea of a joke ? Slowly she replaced the receiver with mixed feelings. Her heart had lifted at the prospect of seeing him again, but her brain was cautioning her to be wary if she did not want to be fooled. He did not mean a word he said, he was an actor and played for effect. He had spoken a good curtain line, unexpected and intriguing, and she must not allow herself to be elated or intrigued. Actually she was both.

Aunt Marion came into the room and saw her standing by the phone.

' Who was that ? ' she asked.

' Mr Marsh. He hopes to come down on Sunday.'

' To see his fiancée, I suppose, but I thought she was going back to Town.'

' I don't know anything about that,' Pauline said demurely, and hoped Viola would not change her mind.

The hope was a vain one. Viola changed her plans; moreover she was most annoyed about the telephone call, she could not understand why Anthony had not rung her.

' It was most stupid of him,' she declared. ' Why, if your aunt hadn't mentioned he was coming, I might easily have gone back to London and missed him.'

Pauline, wishing that Aunt Marion had held her tongue, suggested that Anthony did not realize that Viola was still staying at Melford.

' Of course he knows I'm still here, why else should he be coming when he's so busy ? ' She looked at Pauline suspiciously. ' Who else should he want to see ? '

Pauline said nothing.

Aunt Marion announced that she would not go to church, as she wanted to prepare a special lunch for the master, and presumably Viola, and Pauline was relieved not to have to accompany her. She put on her best suit, and lured by the autumn sunshine, strolled down towards the gate, refusing to admit even to herself that she hoped to see Anthony before Viola arrived, but again her hopes were doomed. Viola's blue car came tearing down the road from Melford before there was any sign of the Jaguar.

Jo Halliday was swinging on the gate; this was not an amusement he was supposed to indulge in, but Pauline was too put out by the sight of the blue car to stop him. Afterwards she was to bitterly regret that she had not intervened.

What exactly happened she did not see. She was walking back up the drive, intending to visit the stables to avoid encountering Viola, when she heard Jo scream. Apparently the car, going much too fast, had pushed the swinging gate ajar before Viola could stop, and Jo had been knocked off it. Pauline raced back, to see the blue car standing stationary in the drive with a dented wing, while Viola, immaculate and elegant, was getting out of it, and beyond her in the gateway lay a crumpled heap.

Pauline went down on her knees and lifted the child's head on to her knee. One leg was bent underneath him in an awkward manner, there was blood oozing from a cut on his head, and he seemed to have fainted. Viola approached and looked down on them with undisguised disgust.

'That idiot of a child!'

Pauline said anxiously, 'I think his leg's broken.'

'It's no more than he deserves, larking around like that!'

Pauline stared up into the hard blue eyes, unable to believe her ears.

'Please will you fetch help?'

Another car drew up unnoticed by either of them. Viola did not move.

'Miss Herald,' she said urgently, 'you'll bear witness, won't you, that it wasn't my fault. I'm in no way to blame for the accident. The child shouldn't have been on the gate, he was a public danger.'

'You were coming in much too fast,' Pauline said sharply. 'Anything might have been in the drive. But do please fetch Aunt Marion, I can't leave him lying here.'

She knew that it was dangerous to move the boy without expert help, but her aunt was familiar with first aid and would know what to do. She was holding the little wizened face against her breast and inexpertly dabbing at the cut with her handkerchief, when to her enormous relief she heard a familiar voice say:

'We must carry him to the house on my car rug, but first we must do something about that leg. If we tie it to the sound one it will act as a splint.'

Anthony was kneeling beside her and stripping off his tie.

'Oh, Tony!' Viola was also relieved. 'Did you see what happened? You'll say it wasn't my fault, won't you? I couldn't bear to have my licence suspended.'

Anthony gave her one look, a look which made

even Viola quail, then ignored her completely. Very gently he moved the injured leg and strapped it to the sound one, using his tie and the belt from Pauline's jacket, which she silently handed to him. Jo moaned faintly and she tried to reassure him.

'It's all right, darling, we'll soon make it better.'

Carefully they laid him on the thick rug.

'You take one end and I'll take the other,' Anthony directed Pauline. 'Keep it taut.'

'He'll make it filthy,' Viola objected. 'I've never seen such a dirty child.' Which was untrue, but dust and fallen leaves had gathered by the gate and Joe and his helpers were plentifully sprinkled with them.

'Go to the house and tell them what's happened,' Anthony commanded Viola, and with a shrug she walked away. He turned back to Pauline and with infinite care they raised the child between them and started slowly towards the house.

Aunt Marion met them at the door, having been warned by Viola that an accident had occurred. After half a lifetime with the mad Heralds, she was well used to dealing with such emergencies. Lynette was spreading a mattress on the floor of the lounge. Viola had been requested to ring for the doctor, which service she was performing sulkily. They laid Jo on the mattress and Aunt Marion considered that it would be best to leave the leg untouched for the doctor; meanwhile she fetched water and towels to bathe the boy's face. Anthony went to find Josh, while Pauline knelt beside the patient holding his clutching fingers; Lynette was crying quietly. The boy seemed to be trying to say something, but Pauline could not make out what. They none of them took any notice of Viola, who stood biting her lip and tapping her foot until Anthony returned with the child's father.

'Come along out of this shambles, Tony,' she commanded. 'There are plenty of people here now to look after the brat, and I want to explain . . .'

'You can do your explaining to the magistrate,' he interrupted coldly, 'when the case comes up in court.'

Viola looked flabbergasted. 'Oh no!' she exclaimed. 'You mustn't report it, nobody need know.'

'All accidents have to be reported to the police,' Anthony told her, 'and there's bound to be an inquiry. I'd better get on to them now.'

He moved towards his own room where he had an extension, and Viola followed him, still expostulating.

Pauline rose to her feet and let Josh take her place.

'That dame in't going to get away with this,' he said grimly. He raised the boy's head on his knee. 'What's wrong, kid? What you want to say?' He bent his head towards the child's mouth.

'I couldn't make out what's troubling him,' Pauline told him, but Josh did.

'There, kid,' he said soothingly. 'Broken limbs in't naught at your age, you'll be right as rain in a few weeks. It won't stop you riding, I promise you.' He looked up at Pauline and she saw tears in his small eyes. 'Darned kid were afeared this'ud stop him being a jockey.'

Jo's head had fallen back against his father's arm and he managed a shaky smile. Anthony came back into the room.

'He shall have the best treatment possible,' he said. He came to stand beside Pauline. Viola, looking subdued and a little scared, had followed him. She hovered uncertainly on the fringe of the group all intent upon the child, while her lips twisted contemptuously. She threw an appealing glance towards Anthony.

'Tony, must we stay here?'

He said without looking at her: 'You needn't. I want to hear the doctor's verdict.'

She muttered 'Ridiculous fuss!' shrugged her shoulders and went out, and they heard her start up her car.

The doctor came and announced that Jo must go to hospital and be X-rayed. He would ring for an ambulance; meanwhile it would be as well to clear the room while he dressed the head wound. Josh could stay, and Aunt Marion. Anthony glanced at Pauline's pale face, and taking her by the arm, led her into his own sitting room. She went without demur, realizing that she felt more shaken than she cared to admit. She would never forget the relief and joy that she had experienced when Anthony appeared; her earlier doubts and scorn evaporated in the sheer comfort of his presence.

She had not been into the drawing room, since Anthony had been in occupation. She had avoided doing so, not wishing to see it changed. Brocade curtains and wall-to-wall carpeting had made what had always been a gracious room quite beautiful, but she was too concerned over Jo to give it more than a cursory glance.

'I was to blame,' she said. 'I saw him swinging on the gate and I didn't stop him. Now if he's lame for life . . .' Tears that she had too long restrained began to flow.

'He won't be lamed for life, and it wasn't you who are to blame. Here . . . stop that, child, haven't you got a handkerchief?'

'I used it on Jo.' She glanced in dismay at the

blood and dust on her skirt. 'Oh dear, my one decent suit!'

'You shall have another.'

As once before he produced his own clean handkerchief with its faint scent of lavender and very gently he stooped and wiped her tears from her cheeks. Then equally gently he kissed her trembling lips.

'Seems to be becoming a habit,' he remarked as he straightened himself.

She smiled wanly. He reminded her of how her father used to comfort her for some childish mishap, when he always 'kissed it better'.

'You're very kind,' she said. 'I'm sorry to be so silly, but Jo looked such a poor little waif.'

'But he's tough. He'll be okay. Sit down while I get you a drink.'

Pauline sank down on to the luxurious settee and became aware of her surroundings. She glanced at the few pictures on the walls, reproductions of old masters, a charming terra-cotta figure on a wall bracket, the fluffy rug in front of the renovated fireplace—a costly affair, suggesting antique brick and tile.

'This room's lovely,' she said appreciatively. 'You must have lots of money, Mr Marsh.'

He smiled at the naïve remark. 'I'm not exactly rolling, but I have spread myself a bit over Three Chimneys, and I had some of my legacy left to help with the furnishings.'

He brought her a glass of red wine.

'You always seem to be giving me drinks.'

'You always seem to be in need of a pick-me-up.'

She laughed shakily. 'You'd better give me your handkerchief to wash . . . Oh, goodness!' she scrambled to her feet, 'I forgot what a mess I'm in, I'll stain your beautiful cushions.'

'If you jump about like that you'll spill your wine and stain my beautiful carpet,' he pointed out. 'Sit down, Lina, I don't care a damn about the cushions, they can be cleaned.'

She sank back gratefully and sipped the reviving wine. For the first time in their acquaintanceship she felt completely at ease with her employer, more, she actually felt happy. He had sat down on an armchair opposite to her and was lighting a cigarette. His face was in profile to her and she let her glance linger on his clear-cut features, and the plume of jet black hair across his brow. He must have looked marvellous on the screen, she thought. He looked up and met her eyes.

'What are you thinking about?'

'That I wish I'd seen you in "Passionate Pome-granates".'

He winced. 'You'd have hated it, it was tripe.'

'Miss Sylvester wants you to make another film with her.'

Her own words caused her in her turn to wince, at the mental picture they evoked of Anthony embracing Viola, but no doubt he did it frequently in private, though it seemed he had no intention of parading his affection in public, for he said:

'Miss Sylvester will have to go on wanting.'

'But don't you consider her wishes?' she asked in surprise. 'I mean after all . . .' She was going to say 'you're engaged,' but at that moment the ambulance bell sounded in the drive.

'Oh dear, I'd forgotten Jo,' she exclaimed con-tritely.

'I meant you to,' he said gently. 'You won't help him by tearing yourself to pieces over him, and he'll be in good hands now.'

' I must say goodbye to him.' She handed him her wine glass and started for the door.

' Okay, but no more tears.'

' You must think I'm an awful cry-baby,' she apologized. ' I never used to be like this . . . until Daddy died,' and fearing she might disgrace herself again, she went swiftly through into the other room where Jo was being laid on a stretcher.

When Viola was interviewed by the police, they were impressed by her, for she put on a very convincing act, expressing her sorrow at the accident and sympathy for the child and his father. Since Jo had obviously been doing what he should not, it seemed a case of misadventure, and that she would escape without censure. The one damning fact, the reckless speed with which she had turned into the gateway, was known only to Pauline, and she did not mention it. She had not actually seen what happened, and she did not want to appear vindictive, neither could she accurately describe the speed at which the car was going. It was not the accident or Viola's driving which had shocked her, but the appalling callousness the actress had displayed when the child was lying in the dust, and that was not an indictable offence. Anthony supported them both during their interviews with the police and reassured Viola afterwards, saying that if the case did go to court the worst she need expect was a fine for careless driving and an endorsement of her licence, unless Josh pressed for damages, but he would take care of that. His manner towards her was so kind and considerate that Pauline surmised he was trying to atone for his curtness on the day of the accident, and she wondered that he could be so blind to her lack of heart, but Viola was very beautiful in a sophisticated way, and could be charming when she wished, and winged Cupid was reported to be blind.

Josh had gone to lodge in Bury to be near his son who was in the hospital there, and on the Monday afternoon Anthony offered to drive Pauline in to see him. She accepted with alacrity, though she was a little surprised that he did not include Lynette in his invitation, but felt it was not her place to suggest it, nor could she bring herself to forgo the pleasure of an expedition alone with him, for she could not deceive herself that it would be a pleasure.

X-ray had revealed no further injury beyond a scalp wound and the broken leg, which being a greenstick break, would soon heal. Jo could expect to be returned shortly with it in plaster. In the meantime he seemed to be enjoying himself hugely, as he was unused to so much attention and was already a favourite with the nurses.

He greeted Pauline and Anthony shyly, being somewhat in awe of the latter, but cheered up at sight of the sweets, fruit and books which they had brought.

'All that for me?' he exclaimed. 'Gosh, it's like Christmas and birthday rolled into one!'

Poor Jo did not get many presents on either occasion.

They met Josh in the ward, who was plainly ill at ease, feeling out of place in a hospital, and intimidated by the nurses.

'Reckon I'm more at home in a stable,' he told them. He would be returning with Jo when he was discharged.

'You must have a taxi back,' Anthony told him, pressing a note into his hand.

Josh looked at the amount and whistled. 'I'll

not be needing all this, sir, and very like they'll send us back by ambulance.'

'Take it, there'll be your lodgings to pay for. I feel responsible since the accident was caused by . . .' he hesitated, 'my friend.'

Pauline wondered why he did not say fiancée, while Josh pocketed the note with a sly look.

'Hush money?' he suggested. 'Don't worrit, sir, I'll not bring a case against her seeing she's your lass. Reckon Jo deserved what he got.'

His expression suggested that Anthony was unfortunate in 'his lass.'

After leaving the hospital, Anthony suggested that they should look at the Cathedral, but this proved disappointing. Since it had been so drastically renovated in the nineteenth century little was left that was really old, and it was the fifteenth that interested him. Much more satisfying was the near-by church of St Mary's with its fine hammer-beam roof, terminating in recumbent angels, and panelled painted roof over the chancel. Thence they wandered into the Abbey garden with its ruins of a once great monastic building.

'That I find difficult to understand,' Pauline remarked. 'I couldn't bear to be shut up in a convent.'

'No, you're not the sort to have a vocation,' his eyes were on the full curve of her lower lip, 'but there are times when I have to placate so many temperamental female stars that I think of the seclusion of a monastery with longing.'

She had to laugh. 'You a monk!' while she thought that was why he was so adept with clean handkerchiefs and glasses of pick-me-ups. 'Anyway, Mullings is secluded,' she added.

'But hardly monastic,' he smiled wryly.

'No, there are rather a lot of females milling around,' she admitted, and blushed faintly remembering her own outbursts.

He moved nearer to her, his eyes searching her face.

'But there's one who compensates for all the others,' he murmured.

Viola, of course, who had sought out his retreat, and discovered his 'pastoral diversion'. She had no intention of affording him further amusement. She moved away from him. 'I think we should be getting back,' she said coldly.

In silence they left the gardens.

On the way home he said suddenly:

'Jo's accident reminds me of something I've been thinking about for some time. Can't anything be done for Lynette?'

'Lynette?' Pauline echoed. 'But her lameness wasn't an accident, it's the result of polio.'

'I think it could be cured. I want her to see a specialist in London. I know a good man who has developed a new technique for such cases and it has been wonderfully successful.'

'It would be a wonderful thing for Lynette,' Pauline said thoughtfully. She knew that her sister's backwardness and extreme shyness were due to sensitiveness about her slight defect, which was exaggerated in her mind. 'She could lead a full and normal life.'

'Exactly what I thought.'

'We couldn't afford a specialist's fees.'

'You needn't worry about that.'

She looked at him eagerly. 'You mean he'd give her treatment on the Health Service?' Anthony said nothing. 'I thought not,' she went on sadly. 'Then I'm afraid it's out, we couldn't dream of letting you pay, that's what you were thinking, wasn't it ? ' A slight inclination of the dark head— Anthony always drove bare-headed. ' You've been very good to us, Mr Marsh,' she paused, realizing this was the first time that she had ever admitted his generosity, even to herself, ' but we can't accept any more from you,' she concluded, lifting her chin proudly. ' It isn't as if we were related.'

' I look upon you all as my family.'

She stared at him blankly. The smooth profile expressed nothing except concentration on his driving; what weird idea had got into him now ? No man in his senses would want to be intimately connected with the mad Heralds.

' But . . . but . . . we're not . . .' she stammered.

' You could be,' he suggested. ' You see, I've never had any family life, theatrical children don't. All my people were in films or on the stage, and my parents always seemed to be away abroad on tour. My grandfather, a widower, looked after me when they weren't there, and his housekeeper hadn't much use for small boys,' he smiled ruefully. ' As soon as I was old enough I went to a theatre school, and it's no life for a child, Lina, trying to do lessons when one isn't on stage, being in charge of a grim-faced matron when one is. I was quite a handsome boy, I'm told, so I had plenty of engagements. The money was needed for my support, the wonder is that I didn't become more insufferable than I was,' he smiled deprecatingly. ' Not boring you, am I ? '

' Oh no,' she was charmed to be the recipient of his confidences. ' But didn't you go to boarding school ? ' She remembered that that was where he had met George, and George certainly had not been to a theatre school.

'That was when my voice broke. I had three years of it to lick me into shape—a painful process. Schools haven't much use for infant prodigies.'

'Funny you should have made friends with George,' she said. 'You're so different.'

'Attraction of opposites perhaps. Due to my deficiencies, I was put into a lower form than my age group. Some of my classmates were great stupid louts who thought only of games, and bullied those of us who had other aspirations. George took it into his head to champion me. Good sort, your George.'

'But he's not . . .' she began, and checked herself. It would be wiser not to repudiate George. He was her line of retreat, and she might need his support in the days to come.

'He's not what?'

'I mean he's been a good friend to us too.'

Anthony took his eyes from the road to give her a quick, penetrating glance, and she hastily turned her head to look out of the window. The country they were traversing was very rural, bare fields stretching on either side, dotted with farmhouses and small villages.

'He's everybody's pal,' he said with a hint of sarcasm, 'but we're getting away from the subject under discussion.'

'Yes, well,' she was glad to get away from George, 'I suppose things were better when you left school?'

'Not much. I was coming into the "Passionate Pomegranates" era. Lina, one thing I swear, no child of mine will ever go near a stage or a studio, and my children are going to have a real home.'

She could not imagine that Viola was the type of woman who would give up her career for her children. Anthony must know that, but he could well afford to employ a good nannie, always supposing he had any children; neither could she imagine Viola as a mother after the way she had looked at poor Jo. From Viola her thoughts returned to Anthony's story, the lonely child driven from pillar to post in that strange world of the theatre which was completely alien to her.

'But weren't there compensations?' she asked. 'Even as a child you were a success, and don't children enjoy success?'

He nodded. 'It nearly ruined me, I told you I became quite insufferable, perhaps I still am. You think so, don't you?'

'No!' she exclaimed, taken by surprise. 'Well, perhaps just at first. You see, I resented you owning Three Chimneys.'

'Don't you still?'

She realized she did not, but she said primly, 'I've learned to submit to the inevitable.'

'Go on doing that and it'll suit me,' he told her, and she sensed an undercurrent to his words. 'So you see,' he went on in a lighter tone, 'why I find your family life so attractive. I've been wondering if you would adopt me.'

'But we're not at all cosy or domesticated,' Pauline told him, 'if that's what you're thinking. When Daddy was alive we were called the mad Heralds.'

'I wouldn't call your aunt or Lynette mad.'

'Aunt Marion isn't really one of us, and Lynette's always been different. Of course she adores you already, though I can't answer for Mike, but if it's what you want, I'll try to be a good sister to you.'

If he wanted to play 'Happy Families' she was quite ready to humour him!

He looked startled. 'Sister?' he exclaimed.

'Well, if we're to adopt you, what else could I

be ? You're not old enough to be an uncle. I haven't got one, but I've always pictured uncles as being bald and benign.'

He laughed. ' I'm not bald yet.'

She glanced at his thick dark hair. ' No, so you can't qualify. You'll have to be my brother—that is,' she sighed, ' until you're married and have your own family.'

' It'll do to be going on with,' he said enigmatically. ' And so, as your brother, your elder brother and head of the family, I'll make an appointment for Lynette to see this specialist.'

So that was what his story had been leading up to ! By devious ways and playing on her sympathies he expected to get his own way, but it would be a wonderful thing for Lynette if she could be cured and she had no right to let her pride deprive her sister of the opportunity. She made one last protest.

' But you said you weren't rich.'

' I've more than enough for a lone bachelor,' he told her. ' Please don't try to deprive me of the pleasure of doing some good with my money.'

Viola would soon alter all that, she thought wryly.

' Then thank you very much,' she said, 'and it's really awfully good of you, Mr Marsh.'

' My name's Anthony,' he suggested.

' Oh, but I couldn't . . .'

' Don't sisters call their brothers by their christian names ? But please, not Tony.'

Tony was Viola's name for him, he wanted only her to use it.

' Anthony,' she said shyly.

Viola came round that evening having quite recovered her poise and self-confidence and anxious

117

to re-establish herself in everyone's good graces. She said she had been thinking about the poor little boy all day, except when the police were badgering her, and she was so deeply grieved to think that she was the cause of his suffering. How was he? She would have gone to see him herself, but had not felt that she would be a welcome visitor. If she had appeared unfeeling when the accident occurred it was because she had been so terribly shocked, she had not been herself at all. What could she send the child? Fruit? Sweets? Flowers?

'Comics,' said Lynette, who knew Jo's taste, 'he's had lots of everything else.'

'Comics?' Viola looked disdainful. 'You mean those vulgar picture papers one sees on bookstalls? I suppose he *would* like those,' then realizing she was slipping from her role of sweet sympathizer, she went on, 'Of course I'll get some. Perhaps you'll help me, Mike, or get them for me, tomorrow?'

'Delighted,' Michael said, then catching Anthony's eye upon him, 'That is if I can find time. I do have work to do.'

'Well, in that case, perhaps Tony'll take me. You know what they are, Tony?'

Anthony shook his head. 'Sorry, but I'm leaving tonight. I've already stayed longer than I should have done.'

They were all in the lounge, where Viola had burst in upon them to play her contrition act, as Anthony was about to say goodbye.

Viola went up to him and laid a beautifully manicured hand upon his sleeve.

'You poor darling,' she cooed, 'what a time you've had, and all through me, but surely you don't have to rush off and drive all through the night?'

To Pauline's surprise Anthony's response to this

advance was definitely hostile.

'I'm glad you recognize your responsibility,' he said coldly, 'but I really must go; I shan't be driving through the night, as you so dramatically put it. It only takes about a couple of hours to get up to Town and there'll be no traffic blocks at this hour,' and he removed her hand rather as if it were an obnoxious insect. Although he had been kind to her when she had been in real trouble, evidently he had not forgotten her behaviour on the previous morning and doubted the sincerity of her present performance. Viola, however, refused to be snubbed.

'Then can't you spare a few minutes to say good-bye to me properly?' she asked. 'I've some messages I want you to take to my friends and I've hardly seen you at all because of all this to-do about that . . . poor little boy,' she amended hastily, seeing Anthony frown. She had obviously been going to say something much more derogatory.

'Sorry, I can't,' he said shortly. 'There's a telephone extension in my room if you want to ring your friends.'

Viola opened her blue eyes very wide and gave him a reproachful look, then she laughed.

'My sweet, you must be very tired to be so bearish. Mike darling, will you see me to my car, since Tony's in such a hurry to be off?'

Michael sprang forward eagerly. He had been watching the little scene with mounting indignation. Believing Viola to be sincere, he had been completely deceived by her acting and thought Anthony was being unnecessarily vindictive; he had not been present when the accident happened. Viola linked her arm through his and they went out together into the night, while Anthony watched them, his frown deepening. Sensing a tension in the atmosphere, Aunt Marion said soothingly:

'Mike's only a silly boy and he's got a bit of a crush on Miss Sylvester.' Actually she thought Viola's behaviour deplorable, and could not blame Anthony for being annoyed, but she knew stage folk were casual in their endearments, meaning nothing. She hoped her nephew did not take Viola's attentions seriously.

Anthony turned to her with a smile. 'Only natural at his age,' he said. He shook her hand, thanked her with his usual courtesy for all she had done, kissed Lynette and beckoned to Pauline as he picked up his case.

'Come and see me off.'

She followed him, surprised at his request. Viola's car was still parked outside in the drive, unoccupied and without lights, but there was no sign of its owner or her attendant.

As Anthony put his case into the boot of the Jaguar, he asked:

'How serious is young Michael about Viola?' and he sounded worried.

'He can't be serious at all, he's only flattered by her notice, she's so very glamorous.' Pauline was trying to reassure him. She too wondered—wondered also if Anthony were displeased. His fiancée was encouraging her brother in a way which he could only be expected to resent, so it was not surprising he had been cool to her. Anxious to protect Michael, she added:

'He must know she's not for him.'

'You're sure he realizes that?' he insisted.

'I think so, but perhaps you'd better speak to him,' she suggested.

'No, I won't do that, in this sort of an affair the

least said the better. Viola will tire of him in time. I know her little ways. She has only one real love.'

He seemed very sure of her, but Pauline thought he was being rather too complacent. She would not like the man she loved to flirt openly with another girl, but stage people were so used to making faked love, they seemed not to mind. The man she loved? But she had never been in love, and it seemed to be an uncomfortable process.

'Perhaps she's only trying to make you jealous,' she suggested.

'I'm not worried about her,' he told her, 'but about him. You Heralds do rather go off the deep end when your emotions are involved.'

She blushed in the concealing dark, recalling the many explosions he had provoked from herself.

'Oh, I expect he'll get over it,' she said. 'He'll have to. There's nothing else he can do.'

'I hope so,' Anthony said doubtfully. 'Goodbye, little sister.' He stooped and kissed her lightly, as he had kissed Lynette, and entered his car.

Pauline stood watching the red light vanish down the drive. She had not enough experience to recognize love where her own emotions were concerned, but she did know that she no longer hated Anthony Marsh, and she was also very sure that the feeling she had for him was not sisterly.

CHAPTER VI

Lynette received the news that she was to visit a
London specialist with dismay and apprehension.
Anthony had had a long telephone conversation with
Aunt Marion, from which she deduced that Dr
Gardiner was seeing Lynette as a special favour to
a friend. Had she realized that Anthony would
have to pay heavily for that favour, she would have
jibbed, as he very well knew; nor did he think that
she would accept him as an elder brother of the
young Heralds, but then, as Pauline had told him,
she was not one of them. He also contacted George,
and arranged that he should take Lynette and Miss
Thorne to Colchester to catch the main line train
on the first and any subsequent occasions.

When Pauline saw her sister depart, wearing her
shabby coat, pale and trembling in George's white
Anglia, her heart misgave her. If Dr Gardiner
could do nothing for the girl, she would have had
to face an unnecessary ordeal. London with its
noise and bustle was terrifying to the shy little girl,
who had not gone further afield than Bury for many
years, and the strangers she would have to meet in
the smart London clinic would frighten her even
more. Pauline began to wish that she had not
yielded to Anthony's persuasions, but it was too
late to back out with the appointment made and the
taxi at the door.

She spent the day in a fever of anxiety, knowing
that her aunt would not be back until the late evening, as Miss Thorne was taking the opportunity of
calling upon Agnes Moore.

' It'll give Lynette a rest before the journey home,'

she had said, thus combining inclination with expediency.

Pauline prepared some food for herself and Michael's lunch, and he came in looking as he had done since Viola had gone back to work, sullen and preoccupied. His sister concluded that he was missing her, and was thankful that the friendship had terminated without an emotional explosion.

The weather was mild and grey. Most of the leaves had fallen from the trees and there had been a marked decline in the numbers of pupils seeking instruction. That had to be expected at that time of the year. Anthony had said that he would not be able to come down again for some time and since Josh had been installed he no longer rang up in the evenings. Often Pauline caught herself looking wistfully at the telephone, wishing it would ring and she would hear his voice at the other end of the wire.

One bright spot on an otherwise dreary scene, for the days did seem dull and dreary with no prospect of anything to break the monotony except the doubtful joys of Christmas, was that Jo's leg was out of plaster and he was limping around with only a bandage, with every hope of it soon being completely normal.

Michael grumbled at his food. Pauline was not an expert cook, and though she could not go far wrong with cold meat and potatoes in their jackets —the apple tart had been made by Aunt Marion on the previous day—it was not an exciting menu for a dull November day. Finally he pushed his plate away and looked at his sister.

' I don't know how you feel, but I've had about enough of this dump, hacking round the lanes with those silly Fraser girls, teaching moronic infants how to stick on a pony, and being paid a pittance at the end of it.'

'Well, what do you want to do?'

He fidgeted. 'I had thought of going into films or television.'

'What!'

'Miss Sylvester suggested it,' he said defensively. 'She's sure I'm photogenic, and if the Spring thing comes off, she thinks she can get me a part in it.'

Pauline was filled with dismay. She had thought Viola's departure marked the end of the connection between her and her brother. Apparently she did not mean to loosen her hold over him, and what— what would Anthony say about it?

'But, Mike, you can't act,' she suggested.

'I haven't tried. Anyway she says half the guys on T.V. can't either. It's a matter of having the right personality for a part, and the looks,' he smoothed his curly head complacently. 'She's going to help me to get a start.'

Pauline stared at him aghast; it seemed that Viola had done her best to turn the infatuated boy's head, buoying him up with false hopes.

'Does Mr Marsh know about this?' she asked.

'No, and he won't until I give him my notice. Promise you won't split.'

'You're not acting fairly by him,' she began.

'He won't find any difficulty in replacing me. I'm not all that satisfactory and you know it.'

She did, but she thought Anthony would be furious if Michael turned up in London as Viola's protégé, but she still did not think the actress could be serious.

'Have you heard from Miss Sylvester since she left?' she hazarded.

'Yes, she phoned me when you were all out,' he

grinned. ' She's arranging a screen test for me, and when it's fixed, she'll let me know. Now, not a word to Aunt or anybody.'

' All right,' Pauline said doubtfully, thinking it was unlikely he would hear anything further from Viola, and wondering that he could be such a simpleton as to believe that he would.

It was dark when the travellers returned. Hearing the car, Pauline ran out prepared to comfort a tearful and over-strained little sister, but the young lady who descended from the car was a transformed creature. To start with she was wearing a new coat, green velour with a grey squirrel collar, and a little grey hat to match; she was flushed and excited and full of talk, a most unusual phenomenon in the quiet Lynette.

' Seeing a bit of life's done her a world of good,' George remarked. He refused to come in, saying that he must return to his garage, and over a cup of tea, Lynette poured out her tale.

Anthony had met them at the station and had insisted that she must have a new rig-out before she ventured into Dr Gardiner's smart clinic.

' As if he knew how shabby I felt,' she said. ' But he's so understanding, he thinks of everything.' The clothes had given her a new confidence, but that was not all. He had come with them to the doctor's and had cheered her while she waited in trepidation for her examination. ' He's wonderful,' Lynette went on, her eyes shining. ' He made me feel quite brave, and there wasn't anything to be afraid of after all. Dr Gardiner was ever so kind, like a father. He's going to give me treatment to . . . to . . .' She glanced at her aunt for help.

' Restore the wasted muscles in your leg,' Aunt

Marion explained.

'Was that what he meant by all those long words ? Well, anyway, he says it'll soon be as good as the other one and I shan't limp at all. Also he said I need building up. That was all fine, but it wasn't the really gorgeous part, because after he'd given us lunch, and Aunt Marion said she'd arranged to visit Miss Moore, he took me with him to the Alhambra Studios. Oh, Lina, he's ever such a V.I.P. !' Lynette's eyes grew round with awe. 'Everyone was so def . . . deferential to him, and ever so nice to me. I had a simply marvellous time.'

'In fact you seem to have been thoroughly spoilt,' Aunt Marion remarked, but she was smiling, well pleased to see the change in her niece.

Pauline listened to Lynette's excited account, struggling with an unworthy surge of jealousy. She was glad that her sister had so enjoyed herself, but she thought Anthony was rather overdoing the brotherly act. She would have dearly liked to see his environment herself, but felt sure that it would never occur to him to suggest it. She sighed. He had always been fond of Lynette in a fraternal way, and no doubt enjoyed impressing her. He was much fonder of her, she thought sadly, than he was of herself.

Michael, who had been hovering, trying to get a word in edgeways, now asked the question he was longing to put to his sister.

'Did you see Miss Sylvester while you were at the studio ?'

Lynette shook her head and said naïvely, 'No, she wasn't there. Mr Marsh wouldn't have taken so much notice of me if she had been.'

Thereafter Lynette's excursions to London became

a weekly affair, but Anthony did not meet her again. He had done for her what she needed, given her confidence in herself, and her trips had lost their terror for her.

A fortnight later, Michael was missing. Pauline knew that he had received a letter about which he had been most secretive. Personal letters were a rarity at Three Chimneys and she suspected that it was from Viola, and wondered what the pair were hatching between them. That Viola was linked with his disappearance she was sure, but was loath to tell her aunt so, although Miss Thorne was worried about him.

'Do you think we should go the police?' she asked.

Pauline thought they should wait a little. Michael was old enough to look after himself and would not thank them for trying to trace him if he had gone off on a binge. In his absence, she went to help Josh, and the little man poured scorn on her anxieties.

'That young varmint in't worth worriting about,' he told her. 'He'll turn up again like a bad penny when he's spent his dough.'

Two days later, he did reappear. Pauline was alone in the office when he came breezing in; he was jubilant. He had had his screen test and had been tried for a part in a T.V. series under Viola's auspices. If he got it, he would be going to live in London.

'What about your job here?' she asked.

'What about it? It's served its turn.'

'Oh, has it?' She felt angry. 'What about me? You wanted me to stay on to suit your convenience, saying you couldn't manage without me, and now you're going to walk out on us without considering whether we can manage without you. Mr Marsh has done a great deal for us, doesn't he deserve some consideration ? '

That she should be presenting Anthony's point of view did not strike her as strange. It was significant of how her feelings had changed towards him.

' You mean he's done a lot for you and Lynette,' her brother retorted. ' He's done nothing for me, you know he hates my guts. If you feel he should be rewarded, you can do it yourself. He's no angel and he likes pretty women.'

' Michael, how dare you ! '

She went perfectly white, and before the fury in her eyes, he quailed.

' Oh, come off it, Sis,' he forced a laugh, ' be your age. We live in a permissive society and nobody would blame you for having a bit of fun on the Q.T.'

' If those are the sort of morals Miss Sylvester's been teaching you I'm more than sorry she ever came here,' Pauline began.

It was Michael's turn to whiten.

' Don't you dare to say anything against her,' he warned her.

' You're infatuated ! ' Her eyes blazed.

' So are you ! '

' Me ? '

His grey eyes, so like her own, were malicious. ' You needn't pretend. You know you're crazy about him, it sticks out a mile. You ought to be grateful to me for diverting Viola's attention.'

' I'm not crazy about him ! '

They glared at each other. Aunt Marion, hearing their raised voices, came hurring in to discover what her nephew had been doing. She sighed when she saw their furious faces; the Heralds were running true to form.

' What's all this about ? ' she asked anxiously.

Michael turned to her with relief; calmly and

pleasantly he explained his plans. She told him that he ought to contact his employer before he made the change.

'But I don't know if I've got the engagement yet,' he pointed out. 'If I do, I will.'

They went out, leaving Pauline to her books, but she could not concentrate upon them. Michael's words continued to ring in her ears: 'You're crazy about him, it sticks out a mile.' Was that what they all thought? Did Anthony believe it too? Of course she was not—or was she? She did not know, but the thought that he might be amusing himself by exploiting her feelings for him was intolerable. She was not an impressionable teenager like Lynette but a grown woman, and at least deserved respect. Somehow she must convince him that he was wrong, though she could not think how. Trying to hold aloof was never successful; he always seemed to find a way through her defences, for when it came to putting on an act, he, by nature of his calling, was much more adept at it than she was. Then something happened to drive her problems temporarily out of her head.

She found a note on her desk from Michael saying that he had gone and would not be coming back, as he had been offered a contract. He had taken the contents of the cash-box and his insurance cards. His behaviour gave her a profound shock, although she knew that he was unreliable, she had not believed him to be capable of theft, for he had made no mention of repaying the amount. She could not bear that Anthony should learn that a member of his ' family ' was such a black sheep. She decided that she would replace what he had taken out of her own meagre savings, and nobody should know about it but herself. She blamed her brother's lack of principle upon his casual upbringing, and she felt apprehensive about his future, but whatever he did, he was still her brother, her blood brother—she smiled wryly, remembering Anthony's pretensions to that position—and she had a deep affection for him, so she would cover up for him and hope for the best.

But although she could hide the theft, she could not conceal his cavalier departure. Aunt Marion was deeply perturbed at his conduct, though she did not know the worst part of it. She undertook to write to Anthony and tell him what had happened, as she did not feel equal to explaining over the phone. Both she and her nieces waited anxiously for his reply, but when it came it was only a brief typewritten note from his secretary, telling them that the contents of Miss Thorne's communication had been noted and Mr Marsh would answer when he was less busy. Evidently he intended to make no move regarding the boy, neither had they any clue as to his reaction.

Pauline resumed some of her former duties to help Josh, and the dull, grey days dragged on. She was glad that Anthony did not come. Not only was she bitterly ashamed of Michael's behaviour, but her brother's words were still rankling. His more sinister suggestion she dismissed without serious consideration. Anthony might stoop to mild flirtation, but he would never go too far, not with Viola in the offing, but it occurred to her that, believing her to be in love with him, he had sought to save himself embarrassment by casting her for the innocuous role of sister. The more she thought of it, the more likely it seemed to be his real motive. It was the relationship girls were always supposed to offer to the men they refused as a sort of consolation prize. With the position reversed, Anthony had offered himself as an elder brother because he could not requite her love. Very neat, she thought scornfully, but she did not want any consolation prizes, and she would show him that he was utterly wrong in supposing that she had any tender feelings for him. There was only one convincing way to do it; she must acquire another man. She had told him early in their acquaintanceship that she was George's girl; now she must become so in reality. Then when at last Anthony did come again, she could confront him with the news of her engagement and possibly be able to show him George's ring on her finger. The anticipation of that encounter gave her infinite satisfaction, without considering that she would have a poor chance of making a happy marriage, for if friendship was not a firm basis to build upon, how much less was wounded pride?

But George, with the contrariness of human beings, proved elusive. He had ceased his evening calls and she only saw him briefly when he was chauffeuring Lynette.

Lynette was now familiar enough with the routine to be able to make the journey to London by herself. She had also got over her nervousness of riding in cars. She had confided to them that it had long been her dream to become a children's nurse. Now with her rapidly improving health, it seemed that she might realize it. After Christmas she meant to apply to the various children's organizations enquiring about her prospects. She had passed her seventeenth birthday, and would soon be eligible. With Mike gone and Lynette on the verge of flight, Anthony's ' family ' was rapidly disintegrating, Pauline thought, but he seemed to have little need of it, since he had not been near them for weeks, and she became more convinced that her interpretation of his action was the true one. At least Lynette had benefited, she would always be grateful to him for that.

Ten days before Christmas, she arranged to accompany George and her sister to Colchester. The expedition would effect a two-fold purpose, her Christmas shopping and a chance to be alone with George. Now it came to the point, she wondered how to broach the subject, but if he were still of the same mind, it should only be necessary to drop a hint for him to take advantage of the opening.

They started in the dim murk of a December dawn, for it did not become really light until after nine o'clock. The lights were still on in the streets as they sped through Melford and Sudbury; beyond Bures they crossed the Stour into Essex. Looking along the valley of the Constable country, Pauline remembered with nostalgia the day that she had spent at Flatford with Anthony in that golden autumn that seemed so far away. Then she had been carefree and heartwhole, or had she? Right from that first meeting in Tavenham Lane, she had been subtly drawn towards the owner of Three Chimneys and that was why she had fought his influence so strenuously. Of course she had not really fallen for him and the arrival of Viola Sylvester had checked any romantic leanings in that direction; now it remained for her to be sensible and marry George. She glanced at his blunt profile against the grey sky beyond the window. He was neither handsome nor romantic, but he was genuine right through, and as steady as the Rock of Gibraltar. Feeling her eyes upon him, he gave her a quick glance and as quickly looked away. She thought he looked slightly shamefaced, and wondered uneasily if his allegiance was fading when she needed it most.

The tall tower of Colchester Town Hall perched on its low hill came into sight, as they ran down to the roundabout where traffic diverged in all directions. In summer this was packed with vehicles, but on that grey December day it was not crowded, and there was no hold-up as they turned towards the station.

Pauline went on to the platform to see Lynette into the train, marvelling how her sister had developed during the past five weeks. She was now a self-possessed young lady with a definite purpose in life. The train came in and bore her away—she would be back during the afternoon—and George drove up the hill into the centre of the town, where Pauline embarked upon her shopping. He arranged to meet her for lunch, and over the meal she hoped to find the opportunity she sought to tell him that she had changed her mind. She paused outside a jeweller's shop, glancing at the display of rings; she wondered if he would buy her one then and there, and for the first time since making her decision, experienced a slight qualm about the wisdom of her action. Once the ring was on her finger, there could be no going back. The street was full of people, like herself, buying Christmas presents, the shop windows were gaily lit and decorated, but she had no gaiety in her heart; she would be glad when it was all over.

Pausing on the kerb, she waited for a flood of traffic to pass before crossing the road. The lights changed, and it came to a halt; across the space now left open she saw George on the further side with a girl. She was wearing a tweed trouser suit, and was like a hundred others, fair hair falling to her shoulders, long legs and a pert, bright face. She was holding George's arm possessively and giggling at something he had said. George's face wore an

expression of smug satisfaction; he had found someone who appreciated his slow wit. They walked
on, and the traffic began to flow between them and
Pauline. She went in the opposite direction feeling
guilty. Perhaps George had hoped to lunch with
his charmer and she had spoilt his day. She was
glad, very glad, that he had found another girl, one
who could love him as she never would, and was
surprised to find her own feeling was almost one of
relief. She had meant to sacrifice George and herself
to her pride, but fate had decided otherwise. She
was thankful that she had seen the girl before she
made any advance.

There was no sign of the girl when she met George
for lunch, and over the meal he asked her if Anthony
were coming for Christmas. She told him no.

' Of course he'll want to spend it with Viola,' he
said.

Pauline went into a reverie, seeing Viola in
glamorous clothes dancing with Anthony, dining
with Anthony, being kissed by Anthony in that
floodlit artificial world of London high life.

' You're very quiet, Lina.'

' Sorry,' she came back to the present with a start.
' I saw you with a girl. Who was she ? '

He turned very red and his eyes evaded hers.
' Oh . . . er . . . that was Kathleen Morris. Her
father is a farmer near Sudbury. She's a sporty
kind of kid—drives the tractor, rides to hounds,
all that sort of thing.'

' I haven't seen her about, but I don't suppose
she gets as far as Mullings.'

' Actually she's been at college, but that's finished
now. Mrs Morris wants her to come home, but she
wants to teach, unless she gets married.'

He seemed to know a lot about Kathleen's plans.

She recalled his expression when he had been talking to the girl.

'You like her very much, don't you, George?'

'Yes, I do.' His eyes met hers. 'Do you mind?'

He seemed to be waiting tensely for her reply. Pauline hesitated, sensing that the simple question was important. If she said yes, George would take it that she regarded him as her property, and here was her chance to draw him back to her. Kathleen had not yet superseded her in his affections, but she might well do so if she did not intervene, and she was reluctant to spoil the other girl's chances, because she only intended to use George as a bulwark against Anthony and felt ashamed of her purpose.

'Of course I don't mind,' she said lightly. 'I'm not a dog in the manger.'

'I didn't mean that,' he said hurriedly. 'You'll always come first, Lina.' Here was her opportunity to assert her claims, but she said nothing, and the brown eyes regarded her shrewdly. George knew her too well not to suspect something was troubling her.

'Ant been making passes at you?' he suggested.

A wave of colour swept over her face and neck, but she met his gaze without flinching.

'Of course not.'

George was crumbling his roll. 'Fact is, Lina, I've been worried about you and him. It was partly my doing he took you on and I . . . er . . . feel kind of responsible.'

'Then you needn't be,' she said quickly. 'Mr Marsh considers himself a sort of pseudo-elder brother to us and of course he's engaged to Miss Sylvester.' Must George too turn the knife in the wound to her pride? But fortunately he seemed to think the attraction was on Anthony's side. She went on, 'Mr Marsh, as you said yourself, regards me as a child, and he and Miss Sylvester are a perfect pair.'

'Now there you're not quite right,' George was not without perception. 'Ant's got another side, you know. He likes simple things, and Viola's terribly artificial.'

'She's an actress,' Pauline said contemptuously, as if that covered everything, 'and he's a player too. They understand each other, and I think it's time we were going—I've still got several things to get before we meet Lynette.' She did not enjoy discussing Anthony and Viola. George had reminded her of her humiliation, and she was half inclined to put a spoke in Kathleen's wheel, but as they went out of the restaurant, he said apologetically:

'I hope you don't mind terribly, but I offered Kathleen a lift as far as Sudbury. She came in by bus and it's a tedious sort of journey. I asked her to meet us at the station.'

She hastened to assure him that she would not mind at all, in fact she was curious to meet the girl, and she looked with interest at the pert, pretty face of the girl waiting by the bookstall.

Kathleen reciprocated, eyeing the slight figure in the rather shabby camel coat with the wariness a girl bestows upon a possible rival. Blue eyes met grey in a long, appraising stare. Nice-looking, Pauline thought, an outdoor type without complications; she'll suit George very well. Kathleen, for her part, was slightly damped. Miss Herald had got something more than prettiness, and she foresaw an uphill task in weaning George away from her, for she had suspected that he had a prior attachment. However, when Lynette joined them and Pauline elected to go into the back of the car with her sister, she brightened up. All the way to Sudbury she kept up a flow of chatter, teasing George about this and that, which seemed to divert him, for Pauline had rarely seen him so animated. Her own spirits sank. Here was another perfect pair and she seemed doomed to be the odd man out. They dropped Kathleen in Sudbury; the short daylight was already on the wane, and George drove the rest of the way for the most part in silence, except for a few perfunctory questions about Lynette's journey, and it was her sister's turn to chatter about all the trivial incidents of her day.

When he left them at Three Chimneys, Lynette said:

'So you've met Kathleen? George often gives her a lift home with us.' She looked doubtfully at her sister. 'You don't mind?'

'Why should I?' Pauline said quickly, finally relinquishing George. 'I'm very glad.'

'Of course he likes you best,' Lynette said naïvely, 'but since you don't want him, I'm so pleased he's found someone else.'

Lynette's tender heart could never bear to contemplate anyone crossed in love.

On entering the house Lynette found several long envelopes waiting for her, the post having arrived after she had left. They were from various Homes, and while she was perusing them, Pauline said:

'Have you thought that if you go to train to be a nurse, you'll have to leave Mullings?'

The girl's clear grey eyes clouded. 'Yes, I know, but it won't be the same here when Mr Marsh is married. Besides,' she added sagely, 'I expect Miss Sylvester will send us packing. Mike's the only one of us she liked, and he's gone. I heard her telling

Mr Marsh when she was here that we were an imposition and a working couple, man and wife, would give him better service.'

'Did you now?' Pauline sighed. 'Perhaps she was right.'

'But if we do have to go, what'll you do, Lina? Won't you come and be a nursery nurse with me?'

Pauline laughed, 'Not my line, darling.' But there was no laughter in her heart as she considered a future which had become frighteningly empty.

It promised to be a green Christmas. The weather was mild and damp with occasional gleams of pale sunshine. Already the bulbs were pushing their green spikes up through the earth, and under Anthony's bay window a Christmas rose was in bloom.

They had decided to spend a very quiet Christmas. It was the first since John Herald's death, and with Michael away, they had not much heart for festivities. They had bought for Anthony a framed photograph of Tavenham Church, and small gifts for each other, but they could send no greeting to Mike, for they did not know where he was.

Then on Christmas Eve, when the short daylight was beginning to fade, the Jaguar turned in at the drive and Anthony was there. Aunt Marion greeted him with ill-concealed dismay.

'Oh dear, why ever didn't you let me know that you were coming? I haven't bought much in, we weren't going to bother with Christmas.'

'Then it's a good thing I came.' He seemed gay, almost excited. 'I wanted to give you a surprise, and I've brought loads of stuff.'

He had. While Josh lighted fires in all the downstairs rooms, he carried in hampers and parcels until their living room looked like a station cloakroom. Lynette was delighted and ran out into the fading daylight to pick holly and ivy for decorations, while Pauline's heart smote her. She and her aunt had forgotten how young Lynette was, they should have made more effort for her sake. Aunt Marion was unpacking the hampers with Jo's help, his eyes growing rounder and rounder as he viewed their contents. Not only was there all the traditional fare, turkey, plum pudding, dried fruits and sweets, but more exotic things, marrons glacés, stem ginger in a stone pot, guavas in jelly, pickled walnuts, and bottles of table wines. Anthony noticed the boy's expression.

'We must ask Josh and Jo to share our dinner tomorrow,' he said. 'We'll need help to eat all this.'

'You would like that?' Aunt Marion was surprised.

'Why not? Jo, you are formally invited to eat your Christmas dinner at Three Chimneys in the ancient feudal style.'

Jo looked at him doubtfully, and then at Lynette.

'He's asking you to dinner,' the girl said, 'and he means it. Do come, Jo.'

Jo looked at the fascinating display of cartons and tins.

'I don't mind if I do,' he announced stolidly.

'Which being translated means thank you very much,' Lynette told Anthony.

'Me dad to come too?' Jo asked anxiously.

'Certainly your dad's to come too,' Anthony assured him. He opened a box of magnificent-looking crackers. 'We'll have fun with these, yes?'

'Them look too pretty to go bang.'

'Oh, they'll go bang all right.'

Pauline held aloof, watching the gay scene with

a queer little ache in her heart. Anthony was behaving like a schoolboy home for the holidays, crossed with a beneficent Santa Claus. He also looked incredibly handsome, the tired lines erased from his face, his eyes alight. It was a game to him, he was playing 'Happy Families' again, but it was very much a family pro tem. Already Mike had gone, and next year they would all be separated. Perhaps Viola would be keeping Christmas at Three Chimneys among a very much more sophisticated sort of gathering. The thought was painful.

Anthony, in the middle of a discussion with Aunt Marion whether or not to set fire to the pudding, looked up and noticed her pensive expression. He came across to where she was sitting on the settle, still wearing her jodhpurs and sweater, and put his finger under her chin, raising her face to confront him. She had much ado not to quiver at his touch.

'Why so glum, little sister? It's Christmas, you know.'

She smiled wanly. 'I was thinking about Mike,' she said not altogether truthfully. 'Have you any news of him?'

He dropped his hand and a slight frown clouded his face.

'Yes, I have,' he said shortly. 'He's all right, but surely you've heard from him?'

She shook her head. Not surprising that Anthony had frowned; Michael no doubt had found Viola again, and he could not be expected to approve of the association.

'Little wretch!' Anthony exclaimed. His face cleared. 'Don't let him spoil your Christmas.' He picked up a large, flat box. 'This is your Christmas present. Remember I promised you a new suit when yours was spoilt? Go and put it on, instead

140

of that rig-out,' he glanced disparagingly at her jodhpurs, ' and please smile, or I'll think I'm not welcome ! '

She dropped her eyes and flushed faintly. It was no use, she could never withstand Anthony. How she wished she had George there to support her !

' You're always welcome,' she murmured softly, which was not what she meant to say at all.

' Am I ? That's the first time you've ever suggested it.' He was looking at her keenly. ' Not sickening for anything, I hope ? You're so subdued.'

She had to laugh at that. ' I'm fine, thanks, just a little tired.' She took the parcel. ' You're much too good to us, we can never repay you for half of it.'

' There's no question of repayment among members of a family,' he told her.

Lynette came up to them, her shining eyes fixed adoringly on Anthony.

' Oh, Mr Marsh, you've given us so much, and we've only a little picture for you which we were keeping till you came.'

' How very sweet of you.' He smiled down at her. ' You're a changed creature, Lynette, and that is a wonderful present, and don't you think you might call me by my name ? I want you to think of me as one of the family.'

' Oh, I wouldn't dare.'

' Does the idea of having me for a brother frighten you so much ? '

Lynette's eyes flew from him to Pauline with an eager question in them.

' You'll soon get used to the idea,' Pauline told her, then added mischievously, ' And perhaps you wouldn't be too scared to call him Anthony.'

Lynette's eyes clouded with disappointment. 'I hoped you meant something quite different,' she said. Pauline dared not look at Anthony; she seized the box and ran from the room.

In her cold little bedroom she unpacked it. The suit comprised a dress and jacket in soft blue woollen material, the dress having short sleeves; there were also two sets of diaphanous nylon underwear and two pairs of tights. Surely Anthony could not have chosen them . . . Viola ? Most unlikely. Pauline felt embarrassed, the gift was too intimate, but she could not resist putting on one set under the dress, which she decided to wear without the jacket, since it was evening; it had all the expensive simplicity of a good model, and she wondered what on earth he had paid for it. She came back into the sitting room with wild rose colour in her cheeks and her grey eyes bright and sparkling.

'Lina, you look marvellous ! ' Lynette exclaimed.

Aunt Marion was faintly disapproving. According to her code, men did not give clothes to girls, but it was a long time since she had seen her niece in a really good frock, and she certainly repaid dressing. She supposed it was all right since it was to replace one spoiled in the accident, and she did not know about the underwear. Anthony's eyes glowed with satisfaction—and something else.

'I knew that colour would suit you,' he told Pauline. 'I sent one of my staff out to buy it . . . and . . . er . . . the other things. Now let's have some festive spirit from you. This will help.

He had poured out glasses of sherry and he handed one to her to sip. Under its influence and the stimulus of the admiration that she had glimpsed in his eyes, it was not difficult to throw off her gloomy forebodings and become gay.

At his invitation, they spent the evening in his room. This had a door at its further end which led to the back passage and the secondary stairs up to his bedroom and new bathroom, the glass door on to the verandah he used as his entry, and if he chose to lock the connecting door to the lounge, he could be completely self-contained. But tonight there were no locked doors between them. They listened to carols on the transistor that he had brought with him, while Lynette tried to roast chestnuts on the wide hearth, in which blazed a log fire, sharing the rug with Duchess, who lay stretched upon it unrebuked.

They were in no hurry to go to bed, and when the clock struck midnight, Anthony stood up.

'A happy Christmas to all of you.' He stooped and kissed Aunt Marion. 'Thank you for running my home so efficiently, Miss Thorne.'

'Oh!' The good lady was immensely gratified and not a little flustered. 'I was only doing my job. Thank you, Mr Marsh, and the compliments of the season.'

He turned to Lynette, pulling her to her feet. 'A very happy Christmas, little one. Here's hoping a new life is opening before you, and thank you for being so sweet to me.'

He drew her towards him and kissed her lips, and she blushed like a rose.

'I couldn't be anything else,' she declared, 'you're so good to me.'

Finally he turned to Pauline, where she sat a little apart from the sofa. Her heart beat fast as he approached her, but when he stooped to kiss her, she turned her head aside so that his lips barely brushed her soft cheek.

'A happy Christmas,' she said ungraciously.

'And you can't accuse me of being sweet.'

'I certainly can't. I wish I could.' He looked down at her from his tall height. 'Prickly little thing, aren't you, Lina?' There was reproach in his eyes.

Lynette was dancing round the room, light as a fairy.

'We ought to be drinking hot punch.'

Anthony turned to her, almost, Pauline thought, with relief. 'I've thought of that. Come and help me make it. It's good to see you dancing.'

They went out into the kitchen together, Lynette, emboldened by wine and excitement, clinging to Anthony's arm. Pauline's eyes were suddenly wet. The little ceremony had been a lighthearted and friendly tribute, gracefully performed—too gracefully; Anthony was excelling himself in his role of the benevolent master, the generous elder brother, but she doubted it was genuine and could not bring herself to respond to it.

Early after breakfast on Christmas morning, George came hurrying round to wish them joy and present his gifts, a book for Pauline, a bracelet for Lynette, sweets for their aunt. They had remembered him with an ash tray, tobacco pouch and a calendar. Anthony, who had risen late, came sauntering in while he made his presentations. He had insisted that he should share the day with his 'family' including breakfast. He did not look pleased to see his old friend and George was plainly taken aback to see Anthony.

'No idea you were coming down, old man. I'm afraid I sent my greetings to your London address.'

Anthony sat down at the table, while Aunt Marion placed a plate of egg and bacon in front of him. 'I wanted to spend Christmas at home,' he said, 'but I didn't know I was to have the pleasure of your company.'

He was watching Pauline who had greeted George with great enthusiasm.

'Have a cup of coffee?' she said. 'It's very good coffee.' It was Jamaican Blue Mountain and Anthony had brought it.

'No, thanks, Lina, I'm not stopping,' George hastened to explain. 'I always spend Christmas Day with my old man on the farm. He expects us all to congregate.'

'Christmas is a time for family reunions,' Anthony said more cordially. 'Lynette, just pass me that box of cigars on the sideboard. Here, George, take these to your father with my compliments, and have a good time.'

'Thanks, Ant, very good of you.' George took the cigars but seemed disposed to linger. 'How's Viola? Doesn't she miss you? I mean, hang it all, it is Christmas.' He obviously considered that Anthony was in the wrong place.

'I assure you Viola would hate to spend Christmas in the country,' Anthony said smoothly. 'I believe she's flown to Paris, but I've been working so hard I needed a complete rest.'

So Viola was in Paris, and that was why Anthony had come; he was at a loose end.

The two men looked at each other, brown eyes meeting hazel with a definite challenge, and Pauline hastened to intervene, aware of a hostility for which she could not account. George possibly resented him on her behalf, but why should Anthony resent George?

'We're going to church, George,' she said, 'so, if you don't mind, Mr Marsh had better get on with his breakfast and let us get cleared up.'

George proceeded to take his departure. He shook Aunt Marion's hand, wishing her 'everything you wish for yourself', gave Lynette's cheek a peck and advanced upon Pauline. She checked her instinctive movement to dodge his intended salute, reflecting that she was doing Kathleen no wrong by accepting it, and acting a little comedy of her own for Anthony's benefit. She submitted meekly to the touch of his lips, then, pushing her arm through his, she said:

'I'll see you out.'

George looked a little startled, and shot a triumphant glance towards Anthony, whose face was inscrutable. Out in the verandah he embraced her again in a manner that boded ill for Kathleen's hopes, and departed in his Anglia. Pauline wiped her lips. Kathleen or no Kathleen, George was still very much attached to her, and though she had used him that morning to demonstrate her indifference to Anthony, she could rely upon him to help her in an hour of need. She went back indoors. In the lounge, Anthony had finished his meal and Aunt Marion with Lynette's help was clearing it away. He was standing by the window, idly flicking through the leaves of the book George had given her, an illustrated volume depicting show jumpers. She wondered hopefully if he had seen her parting from George.

'Thank goodness he's taken himself off,' he said, laying down the book. His eyes met hers, and she saw there was a flicker of anger in their depths. 'I want my little sister to myself.'

The consolation prize!

'Together with Lynette, Aunt Marion, Josh, Jo, old Uncle Tom Cobleigh and all,' she said lightly. Acting was not so difficult after all.

'They are part of the family, George isn't.'

'Not yet,' she threw at him over her shoulder as she made for the stairs, not noticing the perplexed look that came into his eyes.

He drove them to Matins. Aunt Marion had requested that they should go to the small Parish Church that she habitually frequented. The interior was bright with Christmas decorations, red candles on every windowsill among the berried holly, ivy twining the pulpit and big white chrysanthemums on the altar. In the Children's Corner, a tall decorated tree watched over the Crib.

'That's one thing we forgot,' Anthony whispered to Lynette. 'We should have had a tree. Perhaps next year . . .'

Who are you kidding? Pauline thought. There won't be a next year, at least, not for us.

It was a bright, homely service, among homely village people, and they drove home through the bare brown countryside to eat a light lunch. Then, while the three women busied themselves preparing the dinner, Anthony took Duchess for a walk, and inevitably he went to Tavenham. When they were all assembled in their best clothes for a pre-dinner cocktail, he told them that a script was being prepared for the Spring play, which he hoped would be put into production some time during the New Year.

'Which will mean a lot of work for me as I am to both produce and direct it. Alhambra regard it very much as my pigeon.'

'Is it by any chance an accurate script?' Aunt Marion asked doubtfully.

He shrugged his shoulders. 'Near enough. One has to make concessions to the public taste, and one can't afford to be too pedantic.'

'Will there be any love interest ?' Lynette asked. 'I don't like stories without any.'

'Precisely,' Anthony laughed. 'Yes, there'll have to be love interest if it's to have any feminine appeal.'

Pauline sighed, wondering what travesty would be produced involving Mr Thomas Spring, subsequently knighted, a respectable clothier of Tavenham, who died in 1525, leaving £200 for the completion of the church tower, which in those days was a considerable sum. His real life would be far too lacking in incident to make Anthony's film, so action and conflict would have to be invented. Then she caught Anthony's eyes upon her with a quizzical expression, and realized that she was again looking pensive. She downed her drink and resolved to make a determined effort to enter into the party spirit. It was not difficult, she knew she was looking her best in her new dress, and Anthony threw her more than one appreciative glance. The table looked wonderful, and there was an appetizing smell in the air proclaiming the good fare to come.

They dined by candlelight. Six wax candles in two three-branched silver candlesticks adorned the table, they were always brought out for Christmas dinner, and for once she forgot to remember that they no longer belonged to the Heralds. Josh and Jo appeared looking unfamiliar in their best suits, with their hair plastered down. They made no contribution to the conversation, but consumed an astonishing amount of food for such meagre persons. Anthony sat at the head of the table and carved the turkey that he had brought, and Aunt Marion had cooked. He looked very much the Lord of the Manor dispensing largesse to his dependants. And

148

we're all his dependants, Pauline thought, looking at the graceful, elegant figure who held all their destinies in his slim, strong hands. This year it was his whim to overwhelm them with his bounty. Three Chimneys was still a novelty, his doll's house, complete with dolls, to play with. Next year it would be something else.

Over dessert they drank healths to the Queen and Absent Friends, then Anthony produced some old peach brandy for himself and Josh. This had the effect of loosening the latter's tongue, and he began to extol Pegasus and the future he expected from him. A second glass started him singing, and they all joined in a hilarious rendering of 'John Peel', followed by 'Drink, Puppy, Drink'.

'For he'll grow into a hound, and we'll pass the
                                              bottle round,
And then we'll shout and we'll holloa.'

And holloa he did. Aunt Marion began to look restive, and Pauline whispered to Anthony, 'You've made him drunk.'

'Not a bit of it, he's enjoying himself at last.'

Sure enough, Josh concluded his performance with an excellent imitation of a huntsman's horn sounding the 'gone away', drained the last drop of his brandy and rose to his feet.

'Now I must be a-going to bait them horses, but I'd thank you kindly, Mr Marsh, for all you done for me and Jo, not forgetting this,' he indicated the remnants of the meal. His eyes flickered from Anthony to Pauline. 'And I hope your missus'll be the right sort. Mine weren't. God bless you, sir.'

He went, leaving silence behind him. Anthony too was looking at Pauline with an odd expression.

'Perhaps we should drink Miss Sylvester's health,' Aunt Marion suggested pointedly.

'She was included in Absent Friends,' Anthony said without enthusiasm.

Then Lynette jumped up and took Jo off to see her presents.

Anthony had to leave them on Boxing Day, and when he came to say goodbye he stood holding Aunt Marion's hand with an expression which Pauline believed to be of genuine feeling on his face.

'Thank you for a wonderful Christmas, the first real Christmas I've ever known.'

Pauline found this statement a little difficult to credit; he might have had a deprived childhood, but he must have had many Christmases since he was grown up, with parties and entertainments far more exciting than their humble gathering with its simple ritual. As always with him she was inclined to suspect that he was acting a part. He seemed to sense her criticism, for he turned to her and said:

'Christmas should be a home festival, not an occasion for drinking and dancing. This one has been just what I've always imagined Christmas should be,' and she felt ashamed to have doubted his sincerity.

He told them that he did not expect to be able to come down for a month or two.

'But later on, you'll be seeing a lot of me, especially if the Spring play gets under way. We shall be taking some shots on location.'

Which meant that Viola Sylvester would be coming too.

He kissed both girls, those light, fraternal kisses that meant nothing but friendliness, and then he was gone, the tail light of the Jaguar vanishing round the curve of the drive, leaving behind him a great emptiness.

Aunt Marion said thoughtfully, ' It seems to me that Three Chimneys is rather a white elephant to a single man, even one of his means, but perhaps his wife will make it her headquarters.'

Pauline did not think that Viola would do that, but when Miss Sylvester became mistress of the house, she would receive her marching orders. The Christmas that had passed was the first and last that she and Anthony would spend under the same roof.

CHAPTER VII

January brought snow, unusually heavy snow, which
lay over the fields and garden like a white blanket
and not a day passed without more fluttering down
from the dull, grey sky, while the by no means
welcome north-easter swept in from the sea, piling
it into drifts, and far from stirring Pauline's 'Viking
blood', as the poem suggested, made her feel cross,
cold and miserable. The same weather persisted
into February, frequently blocking the roads, and
exercising the horses became a hazardous business
even with sharpened shoes. The riding school was
practically closed and Lynette more than once had
to cancel her trip to London, but her treatment was
nearly over and she was happily planning her future.
Anthony rang up occasionally to learn how they were
faring, but it always seemed that Aunt Marion was
present to take his calls. Pauline suspected that she
was making preparations to move to London, while
she herself was becoming more and more bored and
restless with enforced inactivity. She wrote to the
British Horse Society with the object of taking
examinations to qualify her to take work as an
instructor when the time came, but viewed the prospect without enthusiasm. The truth was that she
was missing Anthony badly; his presence had always
been stimulating even when she had fought him, but
now she wanted to see and hear him with an almost
passionate yearning.

March came in with a blizzard that created havoc
in the countryside, then, having done its worst, the
weather turned milder and the snow began to melt.
Pupils started filtering back, mostly children who

wanted to qualify to join Pony Clubs. Josh recommenced training Pegasus, and in the garden, crocuses and snowdrops were revealed beneath the vanishing snow, while the daffodils were in bud. After the long, hard winter, Three Chimneys was thawing into life again, and Pauline's restlessness increased as the sap rose in the trees.

Then, towards the end of the month, the wind dropped, the sun shone with increasing warmth, the last of the snow vanished from under the hedges, the daffodils burst into golden bloom and spring came to Mullings.

It seemed another sort of spring was also about to burst upon the locality. After a long silence, Anthony rang up to tell them that the Alhambra studios had started work on the Tavenham film, which was to be called 'The Tower That Tom Built'. Both Pauline and her aunt shuddered at the title, which, besides being inaccurate—Thomas died before the tower was completed—suggested the worst form of popularizing a noble concept. He informed them also that a Mr Rawlings was about to descend upon them. He and his assistant were to stay at the Inn in Mullings (Pauline pitied them, the Inn had few amenities), and their business was to make all the preliminary arrangements for the camera unit which would be coming down to take the location shots. They were also to recruit extras from among the locals. Aunt Marion was taking the call, but Pauline could plainly hear Anthony's clear, incisive voice over the wire. Now he asked to speak to herself. He wanted Mr Rawlings to have the use of her office for his interviews and hoped that she would give him every assistance.

'I'll do that.'

He seemed relieved by her acquiescence, and went

on to say that the horses would be needed. ' My production assistant, Miss Pettigrew, will be in touch with you about that. She's a nice girl.' Pauline wondered if it were she who had bought her Christmas present.

' We've arranged a little scene,' he went on, ' where a lady will be riding pillion. I think I remember a grey horse ? '

' Silver ? '

' Yes. I think he would photograph well. You might get him accustomed to carrying a double burden, one wearing a skirt.'

' I know the sort of thing. I'll do that.'

' Fine, I didn't expect you to be so co-operative. No fireworks ? '

' None. After all, they're your horses.'

' So they are. I'll be coming down myself, of course, when everything's arranged. Be seeing you.'

She was vaguely disappointed as she replaced the receiver; it was so long since she had spoken to him and the conversation had been impersonal except for the crack about fireworks. She knew she could expect no more, he was busy on the job and such trifles as sisters were well below his horizon. What she did not realize was that he had done them a signal honour by ringing them up himself about trivialities that were normally handled by subordinates.

She thought the filming might be quite good fun if only Viola Sylvester were not included in the cast. She wondered if Michael had obtained the promised part, but it was unlikely that Anthony would have allowed him to be included, for obvious reasons. She sighed. They had had no news of her errant brother and she had missed him more than she would have believed possible.

Mr Rawlings duly arrived, a smooth, dapper personality, well trained in coping with the hundred and one difficulties which arose in his path in the performance of his manifold duties as assistant director. He was accompanied by a brisk youth who was always referred to as Bob. This individual was always accompanied by voluminous notebooks in which he was forever recording data. They took possession of Pauline's desk and filled the office with cigarette smoke. Once she would have furiously resented this intrusion, but now, since they were a link with Anthony, she welcomed them, especially when Mr Rawlings talked about 'our Mr Marsh', for whom he had a great admiration. He told her that Anthony was wasting his talents in England. He had turned down several chances to go to Hollywood, but he would have to go in the end, for only in America could he hope to reach the top of his profession—a prospect that depressed Pauline still further.

Mullings was excited by the imminent arrival of the film unit, and a steady stream of aspirants came to be interviewed, including the Miss Frasers, who were engaged because they could handle horses. Pauline mounted one of them behind her on Silver in compliance with Anthony's instructions, with a tablecloth draped over her bony knees. Silver submitted to the indignity on the third attempt. Josh was disgusted by the whole proceeding, considering it a degradation of the noble art of horsemanship. Mr Rawlings unearthed with delight several ancients from among the cottagers of Mullings, who, he thought, could not have altered much since the fifteenth century. He badly wanted to include Josh among the extras, considering him to be a wonderful type, but Josh at first was adamant, until he discovered the pay *per diem*, when he unwillingly agreed. He had need of every penny he could come by for a purpose of his own, since he too foresaw changes at Three Chimneys.

Eventually Mr Rawlings and Bob went back to London and an uneasy peace returned to Mullings for another ten days, during which time Pauline received a phone call from Miss Pettigrew, who wanted details of horses and ponies available, and wanted to know if she would undertake to look after them on the set. She too sounded brisk and efficient, unaware that she was interesting to Pauline on account of her proximity to Anthony. No wonder he had been critical of herself when he was surrounded by so many capable assistants !

Then one fine April morning, Michael walked in. He came through the verandah and stood in Pauline's office door, where she was checking her engagement book, and for a moment she did not know him. He was thinner and paler, and he had grown his hair; it hung round his face in a chestnut bob. He wore a polo-necked sweater in a vivid shade of green, and his hands were thrust negligently into the pockets of his green corduroy trousers. But the grey eyes that met her questioning ones defiantly were definitely Michael's, and forgetting all his misdemeanours, remembering only that he was the errant brother she had missed so badly, she ran to him, throwing her arms round his neck.

' Oh, Mike ! Dear Mike ! I'm so glad to see you.'

' That's nice to know, but there's no need to throttle me.'

He reached up, disengaging her clinging arms, and holding her wrists looked down at her smiling.

' Poor old Sis, had a bit of a rough time, haven't you ? ' He kissed her lightly, then fumbled in his trouser pocket, pulling out a bundle of notes, which he threw on to her desk. ' I owe those to the cashbox, and I gather you haven't squealed or our mutual boss would have put me in jug.'

' They don't imprison you for a first offence. I told nobody and paid it back out of my own money, but you shouldn't have done it, Mike.'

He smiled ruefully. ' One of my less worthy impulses. I get them sometimes, and anyway I had to have clothes and other things. I didn't say I'd pay it back because I didn't know if I could. I don't make rash promises.'

She had long since written off the debt. ' You'd better keep it. I expect you need it more than I do.'

' I don't like sponging on you.' He looked wistfully at the notes. ' Tell you what, we'll share it. After all, you don't want much living here."

' Not like London ? ' She handed him back half his tribute, which he pocketed with obvious relief, and she suspected his belated honesty had been a gesture he could ill afford, but it was to his credit that he had made it.

' London eats money.' He smothered a yawn. ' Well, the prodigal's returned and I hope you're going to kill the fatted calf. I'm hungry.'

She stroked his sleeve. ' You're very thin.'

' Haven't had a really square meal since I left— that's suffering for the sake of art. How's tricks ? '

' Well, we're all preparing to receive the Alhambra film unit.'

' Quite, I'm the vanguard. Came down to secure my accommodation. Hi, Aunt Marion ! '

He turned round quickly as, attracted by the sound of voices, Miss Thorne advanced upon them.

' You've a nerve coming here,' she greeted her nephew, ' after the way you've treated your employer ! '

'He's still my boss, worse luck,' Michael informed
her. 'Viola got me a part in this Spring production,' he turned back to his sister. 'You thought
him a tyrant over the riding school, but that was
nothing—nothing to what he is when he's directing.'

Aunt Marion was astonished. 'He's most mag-
nanimous to give you a part after the way you
treated him.'

'I don't think he was very pleased about it,'
Michael sat down on the arm of a chair, 'but Viola
wangled it. Her uncle's one of the management
big noises, and everyone kowtows to her, knowing
that she's got influence. Even old Marsh daren't
offend her, and does she lead him a dance ! "Tony
darling, not that blue light, please, even if it is
supposed to be night, it makes me look like a corpse." '
His falsetto imitation of Viola's voice was excellent
and made them smile. ' " I can't wear that lousy
wimple, it makes me look like an old witch." ' He
laughed merrily. 'It does one good to hear her
when he's been slating the rest of us up hill and down
dale. I say, Auntie, can't you rustle up some coffee ?
I could do with it.'

Aunt Marion did not move, while Pauline digested
his revelations in silence. It had not occurred to
her that Viola's interest might be valuable to
Anthony professionally as well as personally; the link
between them was doubly strong. Miss Thorne was
looking at Michael suspiciously.

'Why have you come here ? ' she demanded.

'I'm in this film, so I suppose I can stay here
while we're on location. After all, it's my home.'

'A home you've forfeited.'

He went to her and put his arm round her. 'Oh,
come off it, Auntie, don't be starchy. Have pity

on the poor orphan. Mr Marsh won't mind, he's too much else on his plate to notice me, and aren't you glad to see me?'

Unwillingly she smiled, unable to resist his coaxing. 'I don't like your hair-style.'

He tossed back his long locks. 'Period, Aunt. I shan't have to wear a wig. Where's Lynette? I heard a rumour that she's a changed girl.'

'She is,' Pauline told him, 'thanks to Mr Marsh. She's going to be a nursery nurse.'

'Well, what do you know! The Heralds are becoming quite respectable. What about you, Lina, still battling with the Miss Frasers?'

'You'll meet them on location.'

'Oh no, don't tell me that, but I'm a player, I shan't lower myself by mixing with extras. Come on, Auntie, what about that coffee, and some cake?'

With his arm still round her, he dragged Aunt Marion kitchenwards.

Pauline closed the door behind them and stood thinking. She was delighted to see her brother again, but it seemed Viola still had him in tow. Would Anthony be staying at Three Chimneys too, and what would he say when he found Michael was back in residence? As the boy had said, he had no other home, but would Anthony understand that?

Late that evening, Miss Sylvester rang up. Pauline, who had been hoping it was Anthony, ran to the phone and nearly dropped the receiver when she heard the husky, drawling voice.

'May I speak to Miss Thorne, please?'

Thankfully she called her aunt.

Viola wished to stay at Three Chimneys while she was working at Tavenham, would Miss Thorne prepare a room for her? Aunt Marion was taken aback.

'I've had no instructions from Mr Marsh about putting you up,' she countered.

'I'm giving them to you now, aren't I?' Viola's voice sharpened. 'He hasn't time to ring himself. Naturally I expect to stay in his house while I'm in the locality.'

'You didn't before . . .' Aunt Marion began.

'Oh, Melford's too far, we have to make such early starts, and Mullings is nearer. Besides, I didn't know Three Chimneys was habitable then. Expect me tomorrow night.'

Michael strolled in as Aunt Marion hung up. When she explained her dilemma he assured her that it would be perfectly all right. Of course Anthony must have told her to ring up, and there would be heaps of room since he himself would be staying at Tavenham.

'Are you sure of that?' she asked, while Pauline's heart sank.

Michael was not, but he thought it probable.

'Well, we can't count on it,' Aunt Marion said tartly. 'Miss Sylvester will have to have my room, and I'll go in with Lynette. Of course he doesn't know you're here, and probably thought your room was vacant.'

'Well, it isn't,' Michael said, and walked away.

Aunt Marion's eyes met Pauline's. Both were thinking it would be unfortunate if Anthony came and found the boy there, under the same roof as his fiancée, but neither had the heart to suggest that he should go elsewhere.

All next day they were busy preparing for the visitors. Though Anthony had still not indicated his requirements, they made his bed, and Lynette put bowls of daffodils and narcissus in all the rooms. Viola arrived in the evening, driving her blue car.

and proceeded to spread her possessions round Anthony's sitting room. When Aunt Marion offered her a meal, she said she would have it in there and Michael could keep her company, as she disliked eating alone. He had rushed out as soon as he heard her car to carry in her luggage, and she seemed to be spilling 'Michael darlings' all over the place. Pauline knew by now that this was common usage among theatrical people, but the invitation to supper was going a little too far. Miss Thorne made no comment, but her face registered stern disapproval.

Mr Rawlings rang up to say that he wanted Pauline and her horses on location at seven the next morning; the extras had all been advised. Viola appeared yawning and flushed from sitting over the fire and asked for her breakfast in bed. Michael, who had spent the remainder of the evening with her, looked radiant. He too had to be in Tavenham by seven, but Viola apparently had not. Aunt Marion watched the reckless pair go upstairs, wondering at what she was conniving, seeing in their behaviour a betrayal of her esteemed employer. Pauline, who did not believe Viola was doing more than amusing herself in Anthony's absence, dreaded the inevitable outburst from her brother when she ditched him.

She slept badly, her uneasy sleep punctuated by dreams, in one of which she was playing lead under Anthony's direction and he was scolding her unmercifully because she was riding Pegasus. She awoke to a grey and chilly dawn, with the bird chorus in full swell outside her window. She pulled a thick sweater over her shirt when she was dressed, and the sun had barely risen when she went out to the stables to prepare her string of horses for their ordeal by camera. Michael came out yawning and in a bad temper to give her an unwilling hand, the

Miss Frasers arrived, thrilled and excited, and a grumbling Josh completed the quintet, whose business it was to conduct the animals to Tavenham. Pauline rode first upon Bonny, leading one of the ponies and hoped the day would grow warmer when the sun gained height.

It was shining on the great buttressed tower of the church as she approached the village, the tower which for five centuries had dominated the surrounding fields and woods, for medieval church towers had also been beacon points, and had so fired Anthony's imagination. For the first time she began to feel some interest in the film in which he had sought to recreate the dedication and piety of a community which had given so much to build this striking testimony to God's glory. Religion had been the core of life in those dim, far-off days. Everything they did and thought was governed by its teaching; perhaps it had been a better world than the present day with its laxity and neglect of spiritual values, but it had not been ideal; cruelty and intolerance were just as rife in it, more than a little supported by that same church which was jealous of any rival. ' All the same, we have lost something,' she thought. ' Could it be faith ? ' Faith, the thing that was jeered at in modern days as superstitious nonsense, faith in goodness, faith in love, faith in God. Faith which still lit many lives, and for which many, many had died. But Thomas Spring had not died for his faith; he had lived for it and left his monument for posterity. She wondered if the actor who was to portray the part would be able to resurrect a semblance of that faith, and his wife—was Viola to play that part, or would she be simpering as the Countess of Oxford ? As Anthony had told Lynette, some sort of love interest would have had to be introduced, some story invented. She only hoped it was not too banal, unworthy of the great theme its director had envisaged. She recalled her own dream or vision on that day when she had first shown him the church, when she had made him see what she had seen. By a curious twist of fate it was she who had first put the idea into his head. 'So he owes me something after all,' she thought, 'though I expect he's forgotten all about it.'

The film unit was collected in a field and among the line of parked vehicles she recognized the Jaguar by its number-plate. So Anthony was there; he must have come down overnight and Michael had been right when he said he would be staying at Tavenham. Pauline was aware of mingled disappointment and relief—disappointment that she would have no contact with him, relief that he would not clash with Michael. She was shown where to picket her horses, and the two girls went off with Michael and Josh to get into their costumes.

It was a long day, spent mostly in hanging about and attending to the animals' nosebags and water buckets. She saw very little of what was going on, and it all seemed to her to be complete confusion. Extras and actors in costume appeared and disappeared, cameras on dollies rushed past her. The sun had fulfilled its promise and threw a bright light over the scene, much, she gathered, to the cameraman's satisfaction. She caught a distant glimpse of Anthony standing by a camera giving directions through a microphone. Never had he seemed so remote. This was his kingdom, here his word was law, and she was on the outmost fringe of it.

Most of the shots were of street vistas, the exteriors of the older buildings (some were old enough not to appear anachronisms), and of one corner of a field near the existing church, where a rough replica of its beginning had been constructed. This was where her ponies were to perform, carrying panniers containing flints and other materials. She saw Viola once, when Silver was called upon to perform his act. She looked unfamiliar in her gown and cloak, the wimple (Anthony had [had his way over that) draped round her head and face. She was to ride up the street to the house selected to represent the Springs' abode behind a liveried servant. Pauline gathered that she was playing Mistress Spring, whom the script had made extravagant, resenting the monies her husband spent towards the building of the church. Most of the interior scenes were being shot or had been already shot in the Alhambra studios.

When at last the sun began to sink, and the shadows to lengthen, changing the light, shooting was declared over for the day. Pauline waited for her helpers to come and assist her to take the horses back to Mullings. It was then that Miss Pettigrew appeared, a blonde young woman, who managed to look smart in jeans and sweater. She had brought her her orders for the following day, and also a message to the effect that Mr Marsh would be coming back to Three Chimneys that evening. So he was not staying at Tavenham after all and would be entering her orbit, but she saw little prospect of direct contact with him with Viola staying in the same house. Miss Pettigrew stroked Silver, said that she loved horses, and looked curiously at the girl whom rumour said was trying to catch Mr Marsh, she did not think she looked sophisticated enough to have much success.

When they reached the yard, Michael, who seemed depressed, went in to tell his aunt to prepare for

Anthony's coming, while Pauline lingered to give Josh a hand.

'You go along in, miss,' he ordered her. 'You look fair tuckered up.'

'But, Josh, you've had a long day too.'

He wiped the remnants of exuding greasepaint from his wrinkled visage.

'It weren't what I'd call backaching work, I'm fresh as a new penny. Get you inside, miss.'

Lynette was full of questions about the day's doings as they sat over a belated meal. Aunt Marion had laid one for the visitors in the other room, which Pauline tried to answer brightly, for Michael was silent and brooding, and the house seemed full of the ominous stillness which precedes a storm.

At long last they heard the car, and then voices in the verandah, as Anthony and Viola passed into his room. Pauline saw the storm clouds gather on Michael's face.

'Has Mr Marsh discovered that you're staying here?' she asked him.

'I neither know nor care.'

She sighed; she was weary and the last thing she wanted was a row. That one was pending seemed likely. They were still in the lounge when Anthony went back along the verandah, and they heard him say:

'Can't stay now, my dear, I have to see the rushes,' and then the slam of his car door. Michael rose and went towards the connecting door into Anthony's room; Pauline hoped it was locked.

'Mike, had you better . . . ?' she began.

He scowled, but made no answer. He turned the handle; the door was not locked, so he went through, leaving it ajar behind him. She heard Viola say:

'Don't bother me now, Mike, I'm tired.'

165

Michael said something she could not hear, then Viola's voice, raised to an unfamiliar high pitch: 'Oh, do go away and leave me alone!'

Pauline picked up a tray and moved to the door intending to intervene on the pretext of clearing the dishes. She knocked and went in. Viola was lying on the sofa, wearing a nylon negligée, with her feet thrust into fluffy mules; she looked very beautiful, and very much the film star in repose. Michael stood frowning on the hearthrug.

'I've come to clear away,' Pauline explained tentatively, but the couple ignored her. Viola threw down the magazine that she was holding and turned on Mike, the carefully cultivated husky voice sharpened to a high-pitched nasal tone, the voice of Violet Simpson.

'How dare you intrude in here! You're only a bit player and I'm the leading lady—it's time you remembered your place. Besides, Tony would be furious if he found you in here, so get out and keep out!'

Michael turned very white, while Pauline held her breath, but when he spoke his voice was low and pleading: 'Viola, you've never spoken to me like this before. You know you're everything to me . . .'

Pauline picked up her tray and tip-toed to the door, as Viola said:

'That's all over, you must stand on your own feet now. Tony and I will be getting married at Midsummer and I want none of you Heralds around here then.'

Pauline closed the door softly behind her. She had expected it, but now the blow had fallen it was nonetheless shattering. Putting her tray on the table, she dropped into her favourite place on the old wooden settle and sat staring into space, wishing

166

that she had not let herself be persuaded to stay on in the first place. Then she would never have learned to love Anthony Marsh. Love? Was this then love? This unrest in the beloved's absence, the embarrassed constraint she often felt in his presence, the few moments of wild happiness? A love that was completely hopeless.

Michael came hurtling through the room and she sprang to her feet.

' Mike, where are you going ? '

He turned his face towards her, pale and contorted with rage and despair.

' To the devil ! '

He went through into the back premises and she heard the outer door into the yard slam. At the same instant, Viola appeared in the connecting doorway looking frightened.

' Where's that young idiot gone ? He said he was going to kill himself.'

' I don't suppose he meant it,' Pauline said doubtfully.

Viola relaxed. ' No, of course he couldn't have done. What a storm in a tea-cup ! '

' He . . . he's very fond of you,' Pauline said dully. ' I suppose it gave him a shock hearing that you were going to be married.'

' He always knew I intended to marry Tony.' Viola had recovered from her momentary scare. ' What else did he expect ? That I'd marry him ? ' She laughed. ' I'm not a cradle-snatcher ! '

She stopped and her eyes widened as they heard the sound of galloping hooves receding into the distance. Pauline was out of the back door in a flash and running to the stable. Pegasus' box was empty, the door left ajar.

What happened next was a welter of confused

impressions; Josh appeared from somewhere, his normal phlegm dispelled. The language he was using to describe Michael Herald was not fit for any lady's ears, but Pauline did not mind. He was expressing her own feelings, only she would have applied the words to Viola. He seized a saddle and threw it across Silver's back, and then George drove into the yard, wanting to hear about the day's filming. Pauline greeted him thankfully, relieved to have his support, while Josh cantered away in a vain pursuit of Michael. Not very coherently she tried to explain what had happened, not only to George, but to Lynette and Aunt Marion, who had come out to learn the cause of the commotion.

'Pegasus!' George exclaimed. 'That brute'll be three counties away by now; Josh hasn't a hope of catching him.'

'Can't we do anything?' Aunt Marion asked, while Lynette began to cry.

Pauline moved towards the stable. 'I'll get a horse and follow them.' She knew it would be a vain effort, for Josh already had the start of her, but she could not stay inactive waiting for news. George took hold of her arm.

'Wait, Lina, I have my car here. We can go up the road, we might be able to see where they've gone, and you'll travel faster than on one of your nags.'

'Thanks, George, let's go.'

Leaving Aunt Marion to comfort Lynette, she scrambled into the passenger seat of the Anglia, and they drove fast up the lane. The ground sloped slightly upwards, and most of the hedges surrounding the fields had been shorn to a low level. It was possible that they might see Pegasus, or at least Josh, somewhere in the distance. The sun had set, and the afterglow still lingered in the long spring twilight, but shadows lay over the fields and Pegasus was black.

They drove in silence for a couple of miles, going slowly, looking to left and right; pinpoints of light began to appear, marking farms and cottages, and the outskirts of Tavenham. Then George braked and pointed. Three fields away on their right the grey horse was visible, standing riderless. Straining their eyes they thought they could see a moving dark figure, and something else, which did not move. George jumped out of the car and ran along the hedgerow looking for a gate; finding one, he pushed it open, and returning to the car, drove it recklessly over a field of sprouting corn. Now they could hear Josh calling, and other figures were moving across the fields. They reached a ditch backed by a stubbly growth of hedge. They could go no further. Pauline was out of the car and scrambling over the ditch and she heard George stumbling behind her. The next field was wet plough and heavy going, but after what seemed an interminable time, at last they had traversed it, and reached the rough pasture beyond it, separated from it by a wire fence which was easily negotiated. George had had the foresight to bring his torch, a big one, and as they came up to Josh its beam revealed the two fallen figures, the boy and the horse. Pegasus had caught his foot in a rabbit hole and come crashing down. Josh was kneeling on the ground beside him, his flanks still heaved, but Michael lay very still.

Now there were shouts and moving lights and dim figures coming towards them through the thickening gloom. George was examining Michael.

'Not dead,' he said, looking up at Pauline, who was watching him with despair in her heart, 'and not, I think, badly hurt. There's a bump on his head, but I think he's only knocked out.'

She drew a long breath of relief, while George stood up and turned to consult the onlookers. After a brief consultation, two of them, big hefty farm workers, volunteered to carry Michael to George's car. Pauline's attention turned towards the other group around the fallen horse. Some sort of argument seemed to be going on, and with a sudden clutch at her heart, she saw a torch gleam on the barrel of a shotgun one of the farmers was carrying. She caught George's arm.

' George,' she whispered, ' George, they won't have to shoot Pegasus, will they ? '

He took her into his arms. ' Come away, darling. If his leg's broken you know it's the only thing to do.'

' George, no ! Not Pegasus ! '

She heard voices raised in altercation, and glancing over her shoulder, she saw a familiar tall figure talking to Josh. Someone flicked a torch in her direction and Anthony, glancing towards them, saw her clinging to George. He came striding over to them.

' Lina, how did you get here ? This is no place for you.'

George's arms tightened round her protectively. ' I brought her, I couldn't leave her to fret her heart out at home. Don't worry, Ant, I'll look after her.'

' Get her out of this,' Anthony said curtly, as Josh called to him. He hesitated for a moment, looking at the dim interlocked figures, then he went to the group round the horse.

' They'll have to put the poor brute out of his misery,' someone near Pauline said.

George said gently to her, "Ant's right, you mustn't stay here. Let me take you home.'

' Pegasus,' she whispered. ' Can't I . . . say
. . . goodbye ? '

' Much better not. Look, love, we mustn't keep
Mike waiting, he needs help.'

Too numb even to cry, she let him lead her away.
This time they sought for gaps and gates. She
walked as if in a nightmare, submitting to George's
guidance, her ears strained for the sound of a shot.
At last they reached the car, where Michael lay on
the back seat. He was murmuring and turning
his head from side to side, but was not yet fully
conscious. She climbed in beside him and took his
head on to her lap, while George slowly and carefully
edged the car out of the field.

Back at the house, the hastily summoned doctor
diagnosed a broken collarbone, slight concussion, and
gave Michael a strong sedative. The boy had
regained his senses, but refused to settle down, he
became more and more restless and feverish. George,
who had stayed with him during the doctor's
ministrations, sought out Pauline. He looked
worried.

' He keeps asking for Viola. Is she still here ? '

Pauline nodded.

' Could you persuade her to see him, if only for
a moment ? It might calm him and then he'll sleep.'

Pauline, remembering how Viola had reacted to
Jo's accident, knew that the actress would not want
to see her brother. Her lips tightened.

' I'll make her,' she said.

The shaded lights threw a rosy glow over the big
room, and over Viola who had gone back to her sofa,
where she reclined looking bored and indifferent.
Lynette was with her, and having told her what
had occurred, she ran to her sister.

'How is he?'

'Feverish.' She looked over Lynette's head straight at Viola. 'He wants you.'

'I shouldn't do him any good,' Viola said quickly.

'I think you might if you said something kind and soothing. Then he might sleep.'

Viola shrugged petulantly. 'Being kind and soothing isn't my strong suit. No, Miss Herald, I don't think it would be wise to go to him.'

Lynette whirled round like a small tornado.

'How can you be so cruel?' she cried. 'Poor Mike adores you. This wouldn't have happened if you hadn't been horrid to him. If he gets worse he may die. You can't, you mustn't refuse, you couldn't be so wicked!'

Viola looked at Lynette with as much astonishment as if a white mouse had suddenly stood up on its hind legs and abused her. No plea from Pauline would have moved her, but this outburst from the gentle Lynette was so unexpected that she rose to her feet.

'Well, I . . .'

'You'll come?' Lynette seized her hand. 'I know you didn't mean it, nobody as beautiful as you are could be so unkind.' She half led, half pulled Viola towards the door, and Viola went, softened perhaps by the genuine compliment. Pauline sighed thankfully that Lynette's tactics had been so successful. Lynette led Viola out of the further door from Anthony's room and up the secondary stairs, which were his access to the first floor. Pauline followed a little way behind them, determined that if Viola baulked at the last moment she would push her into Michael's room by brute force, but Viola went meekly enough, though when Lynette opened the door, she stood hesitating on the threshold, regretting that she had allowed herself to be persuaded.

The boy moved his head on the pillow.

'Viola?' he whispered.

He looked so young, so pale, so vulnerable, that for once genuine feeling cracked the hard veneer with which vanity and self-interest had covered her heart. She ran forward, her draperies floating behind her, and knelt beside the bed.

'Mike, you silly boy, why did you do it? I'm just not worth such heroics. Don't you realize that I'm years older than you are, a hardboiled film veteran who's forgotten what young love means.'

He groped for her hand, and as she gave it, Lynette signed to Pauline to leave them and gently closed the door.

'Where does that get us?' Pauline whispered. 'He's still infatuated and she's only acting.'

'Not altogether,' Lynette said sagely, as they walked away. 'I think Mike'll be more resigned now that he's got over the first shock.' She sighed. 'All the same, I wish Mr Marsh had chosen to marry anyone except Miss Sylvester.'

Pauline could not have agreed more. They separated, Lynette to rejoin her aunt to complete their interrupted evening chores, Pauline into the lounge, where she found George waiting for her.

'Well?' he asked.

'Oh, we got Miss Sylvester upstairs, and I expect he'll go to sleep now,' she sat down, feeling unutterably weary. 'Would you like a drink?'

'No, don't bother, I must be on my way.' He hesitated. 'Lina, love, I'm dreadfully sorry about Pegasus.'

She smiled, a smile that was sadder than tears.

'Poor old Peg—you see you were wrong. He

never killed anyone, it was Mike . . .' she broke off, her lips trembling.

'Lina, I never meant . . .' But he had meant it, he mopped his face. 'All his troubles are over anyway. It isn't all jam being a horse.'

'No, I suppose not.' She was quite calm; nothing seemed to matter any more. 'I've come to the end of the road, George,' she said sadly. 'Peg's gone, Lynette will be going, Aunt Marion wants to go, Mike won't stay, and Mr Marsh is getting married at midsummer.'

'So they've fixed the date? I thought it would be soon.' He looked at her compassionately, while she shrank from the understanding in his eyes. So he too had seen what she herself had only just realized—that she was hopelessly in love with Anthony Marsh; no girlish crush, no passing infatuation, but the real thing.

She sighed, 'There'll be no one left.'

George mopped his face again and swallowed. He thought fleetingly of Kathleen, her bright face, and the flattering attention that he had come to enjoy, but she was one of a large family and had many friends, while Pauline was alone.

'You've still got me,' he said bluntly.

She looked at him doubtfully.

'Have I, George?'

He remembered how she had clung to him in the field and the feel of her slender body in his arms, he could not fail her now.

'Of course you have. Let me get you out of this . . . this circus. Marry me, and I'll do all I can to make you happier.'

'Would you, George?' So she had not lost him after all. 'What about Kathleen?' she asked.

He turned very red, but his brown eyes met hers

without flinching. 'That's not serious. I only took her out because I thought I couldn't get you.'

George too could put on an act upon occasion.

'You're sure she wouldn't be hurt?' Pauline insisted.

'A little piqued perhaps, but she'd soon find another boy,' he sighed as he relinquished Kathleen. 'She's plenty after her, while you . . .' he checked himself. If Pauline lacked suitors it was only because she had not gone out to look for them. 'Believe me, love,' he went on, 'if you could get your heart's desire, I'd be the first to wish you joy, but as it is . . .'

'As it is!' she echoed. 'Oh, George, I'm so lonely.'

She went to him and he folded her in his arms. She found comfort in his close embrace, but she had to be honest with him. Against his shoulder she said shakily, 'You know you'd only be second best.'

'I only ask for the right to care for you and protect you.'

It would be consoling to be cared for and protected.

'Do you remember telling me the world was a cruel, hard place when you're on your own?' she asked him. 'I thought then I could face it, but I guess I'm not the independent type after all. I want a home, and someone to love.'

'Suits me fine,' he said gruffly. 'Then you mean you'll take me?'

She had forgotten about her wounded pride; she wanted him because she felt lost and alone. She raised her face to his.

'Let's be married this summer.' Before mid-summer, she thought.

'Whenever you say.'

He had always loved Pauline, always hoped to

175

make her his wife, now at last he had won her. So he told himself, pushing the thought of Kathleen loyally away. She was an incident that must be forgotten.

As he was about to kiss her, the whisper of car tyres on the gravel outside caused him to raise his head.

' Who's that ? '

' I expect Mr Marsh has come back at last,' she said dully. She drew away from him and stood with every nerve strained to catch the sound of Anthony's footsteps, the possible sound of his voice. They heard him go along the verandah and the opening and closing of a door. George looked at her with understanding in his brown eyes and sighed.

' We'll talk again,' he said gently, ' when Ant and his film unit have gone back to London. Goodnight, Lina.'

When he had gone, Pauline ran upstairs and met Viola coming out of Mike's room.

' He's asleep,' the actress said. ' I think I've talked some sense into the young hothead and he won't give any more trouble. He even wished me joy in my marriage.' She smiled cynically. She was not looking for joy in marriage but an influential husband and a comfortable competence. ' Did I hear Mr Marsh arrive ? ' she asked.

Pauline nodded. ' He came in a few minutes ago.'

' Thank heaven for that ! ' Viola exclaimed, and went past her to the head of the stairs. She was looking forward to the evening alone with Anthony. He had been elusive of late, pleading press of business, but she wanted to consolidate her position with him, persuade him to seek higher remuneration in America, and above all insist that it was time the tiresome Heralds were on their way out.

Pauline went to her room. Leaning out of the window, she saw a light in the stable and remembered Josh. Poor Josh, he must be feeling even worse than she did about Pegasus and was keeping vigil, but at least he should not grieve alone. She slipped down the back stairs and out into the yard.

The harsh unshaded bulb poured light down upon the steadily munching horses as she went into the stable. Pegasus' box door was open and Josh stood in the entry rolling a coil of bandage, with a pail and box of ointment beside him, behind him the light fell on a glossy rump. Surely it could not be Pegasus? Hardly daring to believe her eyes, she crept forward.

' Josh . . . Peg ? They didn't shoot him ? '

The little man shook his head. ' That duzzy fool with the shotgun was all for putting him down, but his leg weren't broke, only badly strained. Reckon it'll be many a day before he's sound again, but he'll make it, or my name in't Joshua Halliday.'

Half laughing, half crying, she sank down on a bale of hay.

' Oh, Josh, how marvellous ! '

' Had the deuce of a job getting him back, the boss phoned for a horse box for him. 'Course, he won't be able to do naught this summer, but there's allus another summer.'

Next summer when Viola would be Anthony's wife of a year's standing.

' I shan't be here then,' she told him.

He nodded. ' Reckoned you wouldn't be.'

' I don't know if the new mistress will let Mr Marsh keep Pegasus.'

' He will if he wants,' Josh declared. ' He in't one to be bridled by a woman, but if he don't want

—well, I bin saving hard and I reckon he'll let me buy Peg and not ask too long a price for him.'

'I'm sure he would, but where would you keep him ? '

'Over at the farm, mebbe. I'll have to fix summat, and a job.' The little man looked faintly worried.

'I may be able to help,' Pauline said quickly. 'I'm sure George would help if I asked him.'

'George ? Oh, you be meaning him at the garage ? '

'Yes. I . . . I'm going to marry him, Josh.'

He was silent. She looked up and saw his small eyes fixed on her sorrowfully, while he still rolled the bandage.

'You be marrying the wrong man,' he said at length, 'and the boss be making the same mistake.'

She stood up. 'You're wrong, you know,' she told him. 'He and Miss Sylvester are two of a kind, and George is my kind, I suppose. At least he's never been an actor.'

She went out into the night, while Josh shook his head and, his bandage rolled, went back to minister to Pegasus.

*

CHAPTER VIII

Pauline walked round to the front of the house. An
orange moon past the full was rising in an indigo sky
and the garden was full of spring scents, daffodils,
jasmine and lilac. There was a light in Michael's
bedroom, and Lynette's shadow crossed the window.
Evidently she had gone in to watch over the invalid.
The uncurtained window in the lounge showed
Aunt Marion bent over her writing pad. Presumably
another letter to Agnes was on its way, telling her
that she would not have to wait much longer for
her coming. The thick curtains over Anthony's
window showed only a chink of light; he would be
in there with Viola, no doubt planning their future
together. She sighed and turned away, feeling too
restless to go indoors. She went out of the gate
and turned up the lane to the left, the lane to
Tavenham. The moon was turning from orange
to gold as it climbed higher, and there was a touch
of frost in the still air, it sparkled like diamonds on
the grass where it caught the light. A white mist
was rising over the low-lying meadows on her right;
it promised to be a good day for filming on the
morrow. She walked on, treading lightly on the
gravelly road, a solitary shadow moving through a
black and white world. A bat flickered over her
head and a rustling in the hedge on her left betrayed
the presence of some small animal, weasel or rat,
about its nocturnal business. Somewhere in the
trees beyond the hedge, an owl hooted, a melancholy
cry in the night. Pauline reached a gateway and
stood looking over the quiet moonlit scene, which
had so recently witnessed near tragedy. Stormy,

reckless Michael! She hoped that he had learned a lesson and would at last grow up. She began to feel cold, for she wore no coat, and the frost was pearling on her sweater. She must go back, now that the peace of the night had calmed her, and she would be able to sleep, her overwrought nerves soothed, before facing another strenuous day. She reached the bend in the road where nine months before she had first met Anthony Marsh. The nine months seemed like nine years. Then she stopped and stared at the tall, familiar figure coming towards her, wondering if her love and longing had conjured up his ghost.

'Anthony,' she whispered.

He was no spectre. The hands that gripped hers, which she had extended towards him, were warm and vital.

'I thought you were with Miss Sylvester,' she said.

He smiled wryly. 'We had a bit of an argument and I don't want to go in until she's gone to bed.'

Over Michael, she thought; he *had* resented the boy's presence, and he could it seemed be jealous; she hoped he had given her a good scolding.

'But you,' he went on, 'your hands are frozen. What on earth are you doing here? Your aunt said you were with George.'

She withdrew her hands at the reminder of her newly acquired fiancé.

'He went home,' she said dully, 'and I came out to look at the moon. It's a wonderful night.'

She realized that she was cold, very cold both outside and in, with the presage of the coming separation and the chilly night air. She shivered slightly. Anthony slipped off his jacket and put it round her shoulders.

'No,' she protested. 'I'm all right, you'll catch

cold without it.'

' I shan't, I've a thick pullover on.' He put his arm round her waist, drawing her close to his side. ' There's nothing like a little human contact to engender warmth,' he excused his action.

They walked towards the yard gate in silence. The close proximity was more than Pauline could bear. He was being brotherly, and she felt much warmer, but soon she would be going out of his reach. A sob rose in her throat, and she began to cry softly. He stopped as a tear splashed on his hand.

' What's the matter now?' he demanded. ' I seem to have an unfortunate effect upon you, Lina. The first time I ever saw you, you were crying, and you've kept it up ever since, but this time I don't think I've got a clean handkerchief.'

He disengaged his arm to search his trouser pocket, while Pauline sniffed.

' I've got one,' she produced it and blew her nose. ' I'm sorry, but you always seem to butt in during an emotional crisis.'

' What's the trouble this time? Michael or Pegasus ? '

'They're going to be fine when they've recovered from their wounds. It's just it's been a trying day and I'm tired.'

' Poor little thing, but you had George to comfort you, and he seemed to be doing it very efficiently.'

The sarcastic tone which she had always hated was back in his voice. She slipped off his jacket.

' Take that back, I'm quite warm now,' then, as he took it from her, ' I'm going to marry George.'

Half in, half out of his coat, he paused to stare at her.

' Good grief, why?' He seemed genuinely taken aback.

'Why? Why not? He's been hanging round for a long time. I told you I was his girl ages ago.'

That, she thought with a kind of dreary satisfaction, would squash any illusions he might have that she was hankering after himself.

'Yes,' he said slowly, 'I remember now, you did.'

A cloud passed over the moon, so that they could not see each other's expressions. He was only a black shadow beside her and she was glad that her face was invisible, and could not betray her.

'I thought ... I hoped ...' he began, and broke off.

She said lightly and casually, 'That we'd bring it off in the end? Well, we've just fixed it up, so my future is assured.'

'Was that after seeing me in action?' His voice was hard.

'Yes, but what's that got to do with it?' She did not perceive his drift.

'Everything, I imagine,' his tone was very dry. 'I'm quite aware that you despise all things theatrical and you consider Viola, myself and all the rest of us as a collection of mountebanks. Aren't you being rather prejudiced?'

'Not at all,' she said, her temper beginning to rise. 'After what happened this evening I've every right to despise ... your colleagues.' She could not quite bring herself to say Viola, and after all, he was as bad; he had condoned her flirtations, though to do him justice, he had been concerned about Michael's reactions.

'You mean Viola, don't you?' he said calmly. 'Your brother will perhaps have learned now that she loves no one but herself. It's a lesson she teaches us all in time.'

So he knew what to expect. It flashed across her

mind that the sirens of history had never been conspicuous for long and faithful love, but they always got their men. Anthony and Viola were two of a kind, they understood each other.

' George is a very genuine person,' she said.

' Oh, very,' he accepted the implication. ' I wish you every happiness.'

Happiness!? Perhaps she would find happiness, she thought drearily, after a time, a long time.

They had reached the side gate into the yard, and she turned towards it, aware of an aching heart. She saw the stable light was still on. Josh must be sitting up with Pegasus. It occurred to her that this was her opportunity to put in a plea for them. With her hand on the latch of the gate, she said, ' I hope you won't part with Pegasus. Josh thinks he'll be quite sound eventually.'

' Would you like to have him for a wedding present?'

' Oh, Mr Marsh,' she turned towards him eagerly, ' I would. Josh can look after him for me— ' she remembered George's antipathy towards the horse. ' George'll have to agree. I won't marry him if he doesn't.'

Anthony had to laugh.

' Lina, you're incorrigible!! If I were George, I'd be wildly jealous of Pegasus.'

' George wouldn't be so mean, he knows Pegasus means more to me than anything.' Except you, she added mentally.

The moon came out from behind the cloud and illuminated Anthony's face, he was no longer laughing and she saw he looked pale and drawn.

' You're tired,' she said contritely. ' I mustn't keep you.'

She again laid her hand on the latch of the gate,

and he put his over hers to detain her.

'May I ask when you and George intend to get married?'

'I don't know. During the summer some time. It would be best if I'm gone before you marry Miss Sylvester.'

His hand gripped hers so hard that it hurt.

'Marry Viola? What on earth's she been saying?'

'That you'll be getting married at midsummer. Aren't you?'

'God forbid!'

She stared at him blankly. 'I thought it was fixed.'

'It most certainly is not!'

'You're hurting my hand,' she told him, and instantly he withdrew his. Bewildered, she went on, 'But she said so. You're engaged, aren't you? You invited her here to stay?'

'I'm not engaged to Viola, and I never invited her here, she invited herself. I could hardly turn her out, could I? Viola Sylvester is my professional cross that I have to bear in the course of my duties. The company find her valuable and expect me to humour her, but thank goodness my contract with Alhambra expires when "The Tower that Tom Built" is finished and I've been offered another job.'

Her heart contracted. He would be going to America. Mr Rawlings had said that his destiny lay there, so that even if he were not going to marry Viola, which seemed so incredible that she could not grasp it, he would be going far away.

She licked her dry lips. 'You're going to take it?'

'Yes.'

'But Miss Sylvester—won't she be going with you?'

'Most certainly not.'

'But . . . but . . .' Since he had yielded to Viola's

persuasions and was going to the States, he could not mean to leave her behind. It did not make sense. They must have quarrelled, presumably over Mike, but she would be waiting for him in the firelit room in her diaphanous negligée, and when he went in they would make it up.

His voice cut into her thoughts and it sounded harsh.

'Can't I get it into your head that Viola is nothing to me but a nuisance and at last I'm going to get rid of her?'

'But haven't you ever been engaged? We all thought she was your fiancée.'

'I never said so.'

'No, but—' She searched her memory. If he had not actually said so, he had implied it—or had he? Her brain was in a turmoil of doubt and uncertainty. He went on: 'I've known her off and on for a number of years, but it was only when she thought I'd become a good financial proposition that she tried to hook me. She's a mercenary little go-getter.'

Hardly the words of a lover, but it was only another instance of his powers of dissimulation. He had pretended an interest he did not feel to keep his job. That he must have been in a very difficult position did not occur to her. The owl hooted again, the melancholy sound made her shiver, as she turned away from him.

'Thanks for telling me,' she said in a cold little voice, 'though there's no reason why you should. Goodnight, Mr Marsh.'

'Wait a minute.' He took her by the shoulders and swung her round so that the moonlight shone full on her face. His eyes, dark pools in the shadow, searched it keenly. She dropped her eyelids, afraid she might betray herself, but she could not stop her lips from trembling. She turned away her head.

'Look at me,' he insisted, and unwillingly she faced him again, raising her eyes to his. He saw in them all he wanted to know.

'When exactly did you decide to accept George?' he asked.

She whispered, 'Tonight, after . . . after I heard Miss Sylvester announce her wedding day.'

'I see.' What? she wondered. Then he added with infinite reproach:

'Why did you believe her? Surely you know me better than that?'

Anger blazed up in her. He had no right to subject her to this inquisition.

'No, I don't. I never know when you're acting and when you're sincere.' All her past bitterness and humiliation rose in spate and overwhelmed her. With wide angry eyes, she flung her words at him. 'She—Miss Sylvester—called us a pastoral diversion, and that's what we've been, haven't we? Mike and I—you've had fun with us both, you and your actress friend, not caring that you broke our hearts . . . all that sob stuff about wanting a family, it was a game . . . a charade . . .'

He shook her, and by no means gently.

'Lina, you don't mean all that rubbish.'

She was too angry to consider her words. 'I do,' she said defiantly, 'every word of it, and that's why I'm going to marry George. He couldn't act a part to save his life.'

'I've never tried to act a part with you,' he said gently. 'My feeling for you is the most genuine thing in my life.'

'Your feeling for me?' she echoed. 'You mean that big brother act?'

She felt rather than saw him smile.

'I don't want to be your brother, Lina.'

'Not after all you said? Anyway it doesn't matter, does it, since you're going to America where you'll forget all about us.'

A sob rose in her throat as she thought of the miles of ocean that would soon separate them, and she struggled to free herself, but he held her fast, his lean fingers boring into the flesh of her shoulders.

'Now what've you got into your head? I've no intention of going to America. I'm going to join the B.B.C.'

'Oh!' She stared at him blankly. 'But Mr Rawlings said . . .'

'Must you always judge me by what other people say? Now you can listen to me for a change, you little termagant. I meant every word I said about adopting your family, but I never meant you to be my sister, I meant you to be my wife.'

'Oh, but you couldn't,' she burst out. 'I . . . I've always been so nasty to you.'

He laughed. 'I hoped that was a good sign—at least you were never indifferent.'

'Yes . . . I mean no. Please let me go.'

'Never. You told me you had submitted to the inevitable, and this was inevitable, Lina.' He pulled her into his arms. 'You're not going to marry George.'

'But I promised . . .'

'Do you want to marry him?'

She was silent, hiding her face in his coat.

He said in her ear, 'Wouldn't you rather marry me, my little spitfire?' There was a tenderness in his voice that she had never heard before, and all resistance went out of her. She clung to him, her arms creeping round his neck.

'Yes,' she whispered.

Then time and place were wiped out in mutual ecstasy as his lips came down on hers, while the moon shone serenely in the heavens above them, and the owl called again. This time his mate answered him.

When they came back to earth, Pauline was full of childish questions as to how, when and where. It still seemed incredible to her that Anthony could really love her.

'At first you thought I was a tiresome, undisciplined schoolgirl, now didn't you?'

He did not deny it. 'But I liked your spirit, and I knew you'd had a rough time. That's why I insisted upon that holiday, though you weren't a bit grateful.'

'Well, I didn't know what you were getting at,' she defended herself.

'My motives were always perfectly pure—brotherly—' he laughed, 'at least to begin with, but after those golden days, I found you were always in my thoughts. Three Chimneys would never be a home without a woman in it—my woman—and I couldn't imagine anyone but you filling the part.'

'You always think in terms of parts, don't you? That's where I got wrong with you I never knew when you were sincere, and then when you let me believe you were gone on Viola ...'

He laid his fingers across her mouth. 'Being gone on Viola was entirely your idea, not mine.' He took her face between his hands. 'You believe I'm sincere now, don't you?'

'Oh, yes, Anthony!' Her eyes were wide and candid. 'But ... but don't actors play with emotions?'

'No, they only learn how to express them, like this, only this isn't acting.'

The demonstration that followed was very convincing.

Flushed and laughing, she drew away from him, and he asked her:

' Don't you know your Shakespeare? "All the world's a stage and all the men and women merely players . . . and one man in his time plays many parts." But need you have played me up with poor old George? You gave me some nasty moments.'

' Did I?' She was delighted. ' I'm glad you didn't have a walk-over.' Her face clouded. ' But I've treated George very badly.'

' Tough luck on George,' he agreed, ' but he too will have to submit to the inevitable.'

' Meaning yourself? You really are a bit of a bully, darling.'

' What a horrible word! I've never bullied you, Lina.'

' Only over Pegasus. Shall we say, then, a benevolent despot?'

' Nothing of the sort. Only your lover, sweetheart, and if I did have to play the tyrant sometimes, it was only because I had your welfare at heart.'

They walked on, hand in hand, through the magic of the night, wrapped in the wonder of their love. As they rounded the corner of the house, they were astonished to see Viola, fully dressed in her outdoor clothes, beside a hired taxi, into which the driver was stowing her cases. (Her own car was at Tavenham, she had come back in Anthony's.) A worried Aunt Marion was on the doorstep, apparently trying to remonstrate with her.

Viola's voice, unusually high-pitched, was clearly audible in the still air.

' No, Miss Thorne, I'll not stop another minute in this dump. I'll spend the night at Melford, and to-morrow I'll collect my car and go straight back to

189

Town. I've no wish whatever to wait for Mr Marsh.'

Aunt Marion caught sight of them and her face shone with relief. She came hurrying towards them.

'Mr Marsh, Miss Sylvester insists upon leaving.'

Anthony was unperturbed. 'Best thing she could do under the circumstances,' he remarked drily, but Pauline cried out in consternation:

'Oh, Anthony, what about the film?'

'We'll manage. We can use a stand-in for the rest of the location shots, none of them need be close-ups, and she won't dare to walk out of the studio, but she'll have cooled down by the time I get back to Town.'

As the chauffeur closed the boot of the car, Viola became aware of them. She came towards them, while Aunt Marion, looking puzzled, discreetly withdrew. Even in the moonlight they could see how anger and disappointment had ravaged Viola's face. She looked quite old, and her eyes were glittering; as always happened when she was shaken out of herself, her voice came shrill and strident.

'There you are at last, Tony! It hasn't taken you long to find consolation, but take care Miss Herald doesn't damage another valuable animal when you ditch her.'

Anthony put a protective arm about Pauline.

'I'm going to marry Miss Herald,' he said firmly. 'And if you're going to Melford, you'd better be on your way, it's getting late.'

Viola laughed shrilly. She drew nearer to Pauline, who shrank against Anthony; her face was a malicious mask.

'Caught him on the rebound, did you?' she said spitefully. 'He's no use to me, since he won't go to America, and I wonder you care to pick up my leavings, but of course you've always been mooning after him, you little simpleton. You and your country home!' she threw a disparaging glance towards the house. 'Do you think you've a hope of holding him? And I'll give you a word of warning—make sure he does marry you, he's a slippery customer.'

Anthony stepped in front of Pauline.

'That will do, Miss Sylvester,' he said in a voice of ice. 'Please go.'

Before the anger in his face, Viola quailed. She spat out a rude word and got into the taxi, slamming the door behind her. The driver started his engine, and the car rolled away down the drive. Anthony turned to Pauline.

'She can be pretty poisonous, but please believe me when I say there was never anything between us.'

'I do believe you,' she told him.

'Thank you,' he said gravely. 'I told her to-night before I met you in the lane that my only interest in her was professional and the sooner that connection was broken, the better for both of us. That was what the row was about.'

'I . . . I thought it was over Mike.'

'Mike? Poor Mike, he's only a silly kid, but he's got talent. When I've licked him into shape, I may make a good actor out of him.'

'You'll do that for Mike? Oh, Anthony, you've been simply wonderful to all of us, and I've been so unfair, so beastly to you, I can't ever forgive myself.'

Tears rose in her eyes as she recalled the injustices she had done him.

'There'll be plenty of opportunities to make amends,' he remarked drily. He drew her close, 'Now, darling, no more tears, the time for tears is over. But we really must go in and tell your poor bewildered aunt that my intentions are strictly honourable.'

With his arm about her, he led her into the house, the house that they both loved, the house that was their home.